Christmas

Grace

Blessings!
Malinda Martin

Malinda Martin

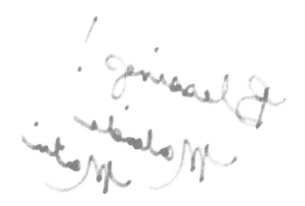

DEDICATION:

To my family who constantly

amaze me with their love and

their unconditional acceptance.

Thank you for putting up with

all of my crazy ideas. I love you

with all my heart.

"And when they saw the

star, they rejoiced with

exceedingly great joy."

Matthew 2:10

CHAPTER ONE

"I hate Christmas," Grace Hudson muttered as she stood alone watching the people of her town gather. Men, women, children, even dogs, all seemed to be enthralled at hearing the mayor's official opening of the town's decorating party.

The Friday night after Thanksgiving was always set aside for decorating the little town. Folks came from all around to add their help, their support, their laughter. Newspapers had called it "downright charming." Grace thought it downright irritating.

His smile beaming, Mayor Scott welcomed the happy faces to the event. "And as we begin the festivities, let me be the first to wish you a very Merry Christmas and 'peace on earth. Goodwill—"

"I really hate Christmas." All right, hate may be too strong a word. But she intensely disliked it. Sighing heavily, she watched her neighbors and friends begin to put up decorations on the main street of the little town of Charity, Florida, population 2,300. Even though she was technically a local, right now she felt she had more in common with an alien from the planet Mars. The Christmas spirit eluded her.

It had for ten years now.

The stars seemed to be winking at each other on the clear winter night. They shone over the town and across the darkened lake from where Grace viewed the festivities. She turned, looking up at the stars, and sighed again wondering how she was going to endure another holiday season without going crazy.

"Dad. How can I handle all of this? Each year it seems to get a little harder. Especially since you've been gone. I just want to . . . leave," Grace whispered to the brightest star she could find.

"Miss Grace! Miss Grace!" A little seven-year old girl came running up.

"Hi, Holly," Grace said gently stroking the girl's golden blonde curls. "How are you?"

"I'm fine, thank you," Holly returned politely. "We're here to help decorate the street. It's going to be bee-you-tiful!"

Grace laughed. She loved all the children that came into her diner after school but she had especially grown close to this little girl. It was like she had appeared out of nowhere six months ago and now hardly ever missed coming to Hal's Place every afternoon after school to see Grace and maybe buy a stick of penny candy.

"Whatcha doing out here, Miss Grace?" Her wide eyes spoke of the innocence of youth.

"I'm talking to my father." Grace smiled as Holly looked around. "No, he's up there," she said pointing to the stars.

"Golly!" Holly exclaimed. "How'd he get up there?"

Grace smiled. Softly she said, "He died a couple of years ago, Holly." When she was sure that her voice wouldn't crack, she continued. "I like to think he's up there now, one of those stars, maybe, looking down on me." Grace looked back up at the bright star she had been talking to. "Sometimes I like to come out here and talk to him."

Holly frowned as she thought long and hard about this. Then with all the attention span of a child, she changed subjects. "Why don't you come help? I could help you put lights up all over Hal's Place."

Grace tensed. After a moment to compose herself she said, "Thanks Holly, but I think I'll stay here a little longer. Now, you run on back to your family before they worry about where you are, okay honey?"

With a nod and a smile, little Holly ran back to the center of the festivities. Grace watched her go, thinking about her own childhood. At times she yearned for those carefree days. Grace fingered the silver star necklace around her neck.

No. There was no way she wanted to go back and experience the incredible pain that happened a decade ago.

By Monday night, everything in the little town of Charity had calmed down. At least somewhat. The tourists would be flocking to the area to see the Christmas decorations soon. Grace didn't mind that so much. It meant extra business for the little diner that she owned and operated. The little diner that her father had left to her. The little diner that she was eager to sell.

Grace was working the night shift, filling in for her Aunt Ellen who had a dinner date. It was late and only a few patrons remained in the diner, having a last cup of coffee and a piece of pie. It had been a quiet night, Grace thought as she straightened the shelves behind the counter and day dreamed of hanging out the "closed" sign in about . . . She looked at her watch. About forty-five minutes.

Just then Ellen whirled in, her eyes bright, her cheeks rosy. Ellen was only fifteen years older than her twenty-five year old niece but looked like she could easily be Grace's sister. They shared the same brown eyes, however Ellen's hair was a dark auburn while Grace was a blonde.

Grace stopped her work to see the woman who had been like a mother to her, come floating in. "Well, look at you! Did you have a good time?"

Ellen smiled shyly and ran her fingers through her hair to arrange it after the wind had blown it around her face. "Oh, honey, I did." The gleam in her eyes sharpened. "Howard was quite the gentleman. He opened the car door for me, took my coat, pulled the chair out for me." Ellen sighed and looked into the distance. "It was like a movie."

Grace smiled. She hadn't dated in so long, she was enjoying hearing the details from Ellen. It was also nice to hear her aunt excited. She had given up so much to help Grace and her father. Grace considered her aunt to be the most important person in her life. With her hair cut short and curled under, she was still an attractive woman. Added to that, Ellen's optimism about life shone through her brown eyes, making her lovely. It was about time some nice man noticed her caring and loving aunt. With a playful tone Grace said, "Well, it's not everyday that a commoner like us gets to go out with the mayor of the town. So tell me Ellen, dear. Did he try to give you a goodnight kiss?" she teased.

Ellen closed her eyes and stood erect. As if she were royalty who was deigning Grace an audience she answered, "A true lady never kisses and tells."

Eyes wide, Grace said, "Then he did! So, how was it? Is Howard a good kisser?"

"Maybe he is and maybe he isn't," Ellen said to the giggles of her niece. "Maybe he has a friend that could ask you out. We could double-date."

This sobered Grace up. "Oh no. No, no, no, no, no. No blind dates." Not liking how this conversation had turned, Grace picked up a washrag and began cleaning a table recently vacated.

Ellen followed her. "Oh, come on, honey. You're young. You need to be going out, meeting people, having fun. Not slaving away at this diner. It's the perfect time of year to be out with others, enjoying the season." After speaking, Ellen knew she'd made a mistake.

Grace's demeanor changed instantly. With empty eyes she looked up at Ellen. "I don't celebrate Christmas, you know that." She turned to scrub the table as her frustration and anger continued to rise. "All I want is to sell this crummy diner and move to New York." The venom in her voice mounted. "Maybe if I 'slave away' at the diner, it will sell faster and I'll be able to leave this little trivial town and get on with my life!"

Then seeing a couple at the front cash register ready to check out, she put on her best smile and went to them. "Hope everything was good," she spoke to the customers as she took their money. Ellen looked with worried eyes at her niece.

After the couple left, Ellen approached Grace and said gently, "Well, thanks for taking over for me. I'll get an apron on and finish up."

"That's all right. I'm here. I'll stay," Grace said, her voice apologetic. She knew that she had stung Ellen with her attitude but it couldn't be helped. That's how she felt. However, she didn't want her relationship with her aunt to be strained. "I'm sorry, Ellen. I didn't mean to snap at you. Forgive me?"

"It's all right, honey. Really."

Before she felt Ellen's pity, Grace decided to change the subject. "Now, tell me more about the mayor. Are you going out again? Where'd he take you? What'd you have for dinner?"

Ellen's reply was cut off as a loud motor could be heard coming down the street. They both turned to look out the window and saw a motorcycle slowly making its way toward the diner. It parked out front and the two occupants, both wearing black leather, climbed off. Grace and Ellen watched as helmets came off revealing a stunning couple, both with jet-black hair. The man put his arm around the woman's shoulder and escorted her into the diner. Ellen took over. "Evening, folks. Just have a seat anywhere."

"Thanks," the man said in passing.

"Ellen, could you come check this out?" Tom, the cook called from the kitchen door. Ellen walked to the back leaving Grace to watch the couple settle into a booth, both sitting on the same side. She watched as the man whispered into the woman's ear and the woman giggled. Grace couldn't help feeling a twinge of jealousy. It would be nice to have that in her life. To have a man's arm around her, whispering to her, seeing only her. Maybe one day. She sure wasn't going to have it here. Even if there were any eligible bachelors, she didn't want to be tied down to this town.

Noticing that Ellen hadn't come back in, Grace walked over to the twosome with menus. "Could I get you some coffee this evening?" she asked as she smiled at them.

Without taking his eyes off the attractive woman, the man said, "Yeah, coffee'd be great."

Grace rolled her eyes as she walked away. She was afraid that at any moment they were going to start making out. How uncomfortable would *that* be? She prayed that they'd wait until they left the diner.

"What a charming establishment. Don't you think, Mac?" the dark-haired beauty said.

"Adorable," he returned without meaning. His hand caressed her shoulder as he looked into her eyes. Yes sir, this assignment would be easy. He'd finish it up quickly and get back to Miami Beach, where he could spend the holidays. The waitress brought their coffee and Mac reached into his pocket to pay for it and then let out a curse.

"What's wrong?" his companion asked.

"I forgot my wallet. It's back in my room." He reached into his other pocket and pulled out change to pay for the two coffees.

"Does that mean we can't have a piece of that chocolate cake?" The woman looked lustily at the homemade chocolate cake sitting under glass on the counter.

"Not tonight, baby."

For some reason, Grace felt sorry for the man. He was obviously a drifter. His black leather jacket was frayed. His dark hair was mussed and long, hanging over his collar and in his eyes. His face had a slight beard, the result of going without a razor for a few days. She left them and returned to the counter where Ellen had gone after her consultation with Tom.

"So, what's the story with biker dude and hot chick?"

Grace smiled. "I don't know. Just passing through, probably. They only wanted coffee."

She began wiping down the counter. Looking at the clock she saw that it was ten forty-five. Fifteen more minutes and they could hang the "closed" sign. She couldn't wait for a hot bath and a soft bed.

"Well, if that's all they're going to have, I think I'll start cashing out."

"Fine." Grace grabbed Ellen's arm before she got away. "But before you do, I want you to tell me more about your date."

"How could you have forgotten your wallet?"

"Chill, Janet," Mac whispered to her. "I guess it's in my other pants pocket. It's no big deal. We'll just have coffee." He smiled seductively at her. "We'll have dessert later."

Janet looked again at the chocolate cake. Dessert with Mac or dessert with chocolate. A tough decision. She sighed. "Okay," she said as she sipped her coffee.

"This coffee is good," Mac murmured enjoying the hot liquid gliding down his raw throat. "Just what I needed." Mac turned his attention back to the woman. "So, you ready to be my assistant, honey?"

Janet was deep in thought. "Huh? Oh, sure. Now how long did you say we were going to be here?"

"I don't know. Until I get what I came for."

"And then we'll head back to Miami Beach?"

"That's what you want, isn't it?"

What she really wanted at that moment was a slice of the chocolate cake. She looked at Mac, enjoying his coffee. He was cute and fun. But anyone who couldn't even pay for her a dessert was probably not worthy of her. She took a sip of her coffee and began making plans in her mind.

"Ellen," Grace interrupted the date story. "What are we going to do with the chocolate cake after closing tonight?"

"Throw it away. Why?"

Without answering, Grace walked over and sliced two large pieces of the cake. Placing them on dishes with forks, she walked over to Mac and Janet and placed the desserts in front of them.

Mac looked up and said, "We didn't order any cake, Miss." He stopped short as he stared into the biggest, saddest eyes that he had ever seen.

The waitress smiled slightly, the humor not reaching those brown eyes and said, "That's all right. It's on the house."

Janet squealed with delight. "Oh boy!" she exclaimed as she dug into the luscious dessert.

Mac couldn't tear himself away from those eyes. "I don't want to get you in trouble with your boss," he said softly.

Her smiled widened. Still her eyes were sad. "No problem." And she left the two alone.

Mac looked down at his cake. The waitress knew he didn't have the money to pay for dessert. Why did she do this? Mac shrugged and began eating the cake. He'd bring the money for the desserts tomorrow. Maybe this was simply what you got from a small town in Florida—Southern hospitality.

After quickly finishing her cake, Janet excused herself to the restroom. Mac lingered over his dessert. It had been a long time since he had relaxed over a slice of homemade cake. It had been close to a year. He smiled remembering. He'd have to make sure that this Christmas was special. It's what she'd have wanted.

Laughter came from the counter. Mac turned to look at the two women deep in conversation. The one who had brought their coffee and cake was laughing at whatever the other one had been saying. While Janet was gone, he took a moment to look at the young woman. Probably mid to upper twenties. Straight, blonde hair pulled back into a ponytail. High cheekbones, slender nose. The smile on her face softened her rose colored lips. But those eyes! He couldn't get past the beauty and the pathos of her eyes.

Studying people was a part of his job and he was good at it. He could tell that the girl carried around a heavy burden with her. Yet she was kind enough to give strangers food without charging them. There was a story behind this woman and he was surprised that he was eager to know it. Then he saw her laugh. It was a gentle laugh, lovely and sincere. It was infectious. Mac wanted to laugh with her.

Mac looked down at his watch. He needed to get back to the hotel and start planning his time here. What could be keeping Janet?

Grace returned with the coffee pot to freshen his cup. He smiled up at her and said, "The cake was excellent. Please tell the baker for me."

Grinning, Grace said, "That would be me. You're very welcome." She looked down to see Mac looking up at her. His smile was stunning and took Grace by surprise. The face that stared at her was unlike any she had ever seen. His eyes were blue, his face tanned and handsome, just like a movie star. And his smile was dazzling. His teeth were straight and white. So white, Grace felt that at any moment she would see a gleam popping from them. His smile brightened his whole face, causing a kind of radiance. Grace thought it was beautiful.

Mac evidently didn't notice Grace's frozen state and said, "No kidding. You really made that cake?"

"Yes," Grace croaked out. She felt a burn on her cheeks as she mentally kicked herself for staring at the poor man. She definitely needed that bath and bed. She was suffering from extreme exhaustion. With Tom cleaning the kitchen and Ellen cashing out the register, Grace resigned herself to the fact that she would have to finish waiting on the man and his girl. Where was the girl?

"Could I get you anything else?" Grace asked standing straight, the coffee pot in front of her, almost as a shield. Mac shook his head and watched as Grace stacked the two plates and forks with one hand.

Taking a deep breath Grace asked, "You just passing through?"

"Pretty much. I'll be here for a few days. If the rest of the food is as good as the cake, I'll be back."

"It is," she assured him.

Mac looked around. "Hey, have you seen the girl I came in with? She's been in that restroom a long time."

"I'll go check for you." After dropping the dishes off in the kitchen, Grace walked to the bathroom and stuck her head inside. "Hello?" Nothing. She walked back to Ellen at the cash register and asked, "Have you seen the girl that came in with biker dude?"

"Hot chick left a few minutes ago," Ellen said as she filled out a deposit slip. "She sneaked out the front door when you were talking to the guy."

"Oh, my." Grace walked back to Mac's table. She worried her hands together as she spoke. "I'm afraid your . . . 'friend' left."

"What?" Mac stared straight ahead and then frowned. "No, no, no." He got up and ran out of the diner and jumped on his bike. With a loud roar, he zoomed down the street and drove to the small hotel in the town.

Through the front windows Grace watched him go. "Poor guy," she said under her breath.

Mac raced to his hotel room, frantically working the key to open the door. He ran to the jeans he'd left on the bed, searching every pocket. Pulling out his wallet, he looked into it. Just as he expected. Empty.

Pulling out his cell phone, Mac placed a call. After the answering machine started he spoke. "Hey, Paula, it's me. I've run into some trouble here in Charity. Nothing connected with the job. That's still on. "Hey could you wire me some cash?"

CHAPTER TWO

Mac was angry. Seething angry. Too angry to sleep angry. He tossed and turned all night wondering how Janet could have done such a thing. True he hadn't known her that long. True he'd met her in a bar in Miami Beach. True she wasn't the brightest bulb in the bunch. But come on. Robbing him and splitting town? He was even angrier that he never saw it coming.

Sleep had eluded him as he tried to figure out how to do his work without an assistant. Without money, for that matter. Well, that shouldn't be a problem. His partner would wire him some cash as soon as she heard his message. Hopefully.

By five o'clock in the morning, Mac was tired of working so hard to try to sleep. He dressed in jeans and a Miami Dolphins sweatshirt, grabbed a camera, along with his jacket, and went for a walk.

You could never tell what the winter weather in central Florida would be like. It could be near freezing or it could be shorts and tee shirt time. Walking onto the street, Mac was glad he had chosen the sweatshirt. His eyes watered as the coolness of the air hit him and he hung his camera around his neck so he could quickly push his ungloved hands into his pockets. He could see his breath expel through the streetlights that still burned. "Northern weather!" the Miami native scoffed.

The sun had yet to rise which caused Mac to enjoy the brilliance of the Christmas lights, something he had not taken time to do the previous night. "Incredible!" His hands immediately came out of his pockets and he began snapping away.

My job here's going to be a piece of cake, he thought as he framed and clicked. His deadline of the end of the year was a sure thing for him now that he had found the town of Charity.

Heading down the main street, his admiration of the little town grew dramatically. Shops, offices, and restaurants lined the street, all decked out for the season. The buildings were outlined in white lights, but that's where the uniformity ended. Each business decorated in a different style making the street seem like a bunch of beautifully wrapped Christmas presents. The Italian restaurant had Christmas trees decorated with ornaments of red, white, and green, for the Italian flag. The toy store was crammed with every imaginable toy, a big red bow attached to each. Mac found himself mesmerized at the blend of old toys, such as vintage teddy bears, and new, like the latest gaming systems. As he clicked pictures, he wondered when he'd have a chance to sneak back and . . . investigate.

A small bookstore displayed classic Christmas stories. Prominent in the front of the window was a small nativity set complete with a hanging star over it. Books about the first

Christmas surrounded the display, some new and some very old. Mac smiled as he recognized one in particular that had been read to him as a boy.

The sun was now peeking over the horizon of the large lake that rested at the end of the brightly decorated street. In front of the lake sat the little diner from the previous night. It was a small building that looked like a train car. "Cute," Mac said as he approached it. On the top was a sign that read "Hal's Place" in blue letters. The building was gray with blue trim surrounding the windows that covered the front. Two doors flanked the building, one being the entrance and the other the emergency exit. Each door was lit up and had four steps leading up to it. Security lights were seen inside. But . . .

No Christmas lights. Nowhere on the building. Mac looked around at the wonderland the little town had created and then looked back at the diner. He frowned and shook his head, thinking it had to be a mistake. It just didn't seem right.

And it would greatly complicate Mac's plans.

Wait a minute, he thought. The lights were probably turned off when they closed up for the night. Maybe not everyone keeps them on all night. Did the place have lights on last night? Mac was usually observant about that. That's what he got for paying too much attention to a female.

As he walked closer to the diner he was stunned to find out that there were no Christmas lights on the place. No Christmas trees, no garland, no anything. Shock had him frozen in place as he stared at the darkened building "Well, this is definitely going to have to change," he muttered to himself.

Seeing a trail that encircled the lake, Mac started to walk, thinking he could organize his thoughts. He had found his perfect photograph—the charming diner with the lake in the background and the beautiful Main Street stores framing it. But in order to get that photo, that little diner had to be decked out. He was sure that he could talk the owner into his plans, he thought as his mind ran wild with unique ways to decorate the diner.

Walking down the trail, Mac looked back at the beauty of the little town. By habit he began snapping pictures. He looked further down the trail and saw a lone runner. The runner was sprinting for all he was worth. It looked like someone was chasing him . . . or her. Yes, it was definitely a female. He could see long, slim legs below running shorts. A light jacket was zipped up over a trim waist. Blonde hair pulled into a ponytail swished back and forth behind her.

Mac sat on a nearby bench and continued to take pictures. He zoomed in on the face of the runner. It was the waitress from the night before. The intensity of her expression amazed Mac as he continued clicking his camera. When she got closer, he hid his camera inside his jacket and waited for just the right moment to speak.

"What's your hurry?" he said as she raced past him.

Grace stopped in her tracks as she recognized the voice behind the blur. She turned and looked at him. He sat there in jeans so old they were almost white. The jacket was the same frayed one from the previous night. Her heart went out to him. Walking back she said, "Oh, just out for a morning stroll. How about you?" Did he have a place to stay? Had he been on the bench all night? She determined that she was going to make sure he got breakfast.

"The weather was too nice to stay indoors. Thought I'd look for migrating birds." Then looking at her from head to toe he added, "Looks like I found a long legged variety."

She chuckled and then put a leg on the bench to stretch out. Mac sighed inwardly. Yes, those were some glorious stems.

"Migrating is a good word. Although I'm actually migrating north."

"What do you mean?" Mac's attention went back to her face.

Grace stretched the other leg. "I'm heading to New York just as soon as possible."

"What, and leave Christmas Central?" Mac said as he motioned to the small decorated downtown.

Grace's face closed up as she sat on the bench next to Mac. "Just as soon as possible." She pulled a small water bottle out of a zippered compartment on her jacket. Before she took a sip she looked over at Mac with sympathy. "Would you like a drink?"

The look confused Mac. He frowned and said, "No, thank you." Then he added, "You know, I couldn't help but notice that the diner is the only place in town that's not decorated for the holidays."

"That's right," she replied, taking a long drink.

After waiting for some explanation, Mac finally said, "Any idea why the owner is such a Scrooge?"

Grace smiled at this. It wasn't the first time she had been called Scrooge and it for sure wouldn't be the last time either. "The owner doesn't celebrate Christmas."

"No!" Mac couldn't believe his ears.

"Yeah, it's true. But don't worry. The diner's for sale so I'm sure that whoever buys it will probably conform to the town's ideas on holiday lighting." Grace took another soothing drink of water, easing her dry throat. Whether it was from running or the discussion of Christmas she wasn't sure. After wiping her mouth with her hand she said, "You don't happen to know anyone who would want to buy a diner in a little dinky town like Charity, do you?"

Mac shrugged. "Sorry."

She knew he wouldn't but didn't think it hurt to ask. "Oh well." She stood up to leave. "Hey, how about I buy you breakfast. I'm heading over to the diner now.

Mac stood with her. "You don't need to-"

"No really. I'd like to." She indicated with her head for him to follow her, which he did with a smile.

After a slight hesitation, Grace said, "I take it, things didn't go so well with your girl last night?"

Mac lifted his eyebrows and stuck his hands in his pockets. "It went peachy. She stole my money and credit cards and skipped town." Grace was surprised the man even had credit cards.

Mac ran his fingers through his thick black hair, pushing it out of his eyes. "In the long run I guess she did me a favor. Good to find out now, right?"

"I guess so." They walked on in silence. Then Grace said, "My name's Grace, by the way. Grace Hudson." She stuck out her hand to shake his.

"Mac."

Grace stopped, still shaking his hand and looked at him. "Just 'Mac?'"

He smiled. The last thing he needed right now was for anyone in the town of Charity to know who he was. Looking into her big, imploring eyes, he decided to chance it with Grace. "It's Mac McCrae. Nice to meet you, Grace."

His hand felt confident and strong in hers. And there was that bright smile again. Even in the cool temperatures of the morning, his smile warmed her clear down to her toes. Grace couldn't help returning the smile.

The diner was still closed when they reached it, although there was plenty of activity seen through the large windows. "Hal's Place" was busy getting ready for the breakfast crowd. Grace pulled out a key and opened the door. She nodded to the two older men that sat on the bench in front of the diner. The men waved back and muffled a "Morning" to Grace. Then they raised a hand to Mac. The elder of the two said, "Have a nice day, son." Amused, Mac waved back and said, "Yeah, you too." Then holding the door open for Grace said, "Who was that?"

"Huh? Oh, that was Big Jed," Grace said entering the diner.

"And who was the other fellow?"

"His son, Little Jed."

Mac stopped her with his hand. "You got to be kidding. The guy must weigh two fifty."

"You obviously weren't raised in the South."

"Miami Beach," he challenged.

"Like I said, you weren't raised in the South. When a woman gives birth to the first male child, typically she names him after the father. From then on it's 'Big Whatever' for the father and 'Little Whatever' for the son."

Mac was fascinated. "So, if I had a son, he'd be known as 'Little Mac?'" Grace nodded. "Then I'd be what . . . a Big Mac?" Grace laughed.

Ellen was back at the cash register, just where Mac had last seen her the night before. Her smile was wide, enjoying the laughter of her niece as Mac and Grace walked over to her.

Mac couldn't resist saying, "Haven't you finished counting that money yet?"

Ellen looked up at the man. She chuckled and said, "I just can't get enough of my boyfriend . . . 'Cash.'" Mac chuckled along with her. "Did you find that girl from last night?"

Mac cleared his throat. "Not exactly. She decided she wanted to move to another town. With *my* friend, Cash."

"Oh, no. Did you call the police?"

"Don't worry about it. I cancelled the cards. She's already spent the dough. No big deal."

"I thought I'd treat him to breakfast this morning, since he had a hard night," Grace explained.

Ellen brightened. "Great idea. The Spinuccis' are making their special Southern buttermilk pancakes today."

"The Spinuccis?" Mac asked.

"They're the day cooks—a wonderful Italian couple that work together," Grace explained.

"An Italian couple making Southern buttermilk pancakes?"

"They add a dash of garlic to the batter," Grace said. Mac snickered.

Ellen interceded. "Now you two come on and sit down. I'll get you some breakfast."

"But you're not opened yet. I don't want to cause any trouble," Mac said.

Looking at Grace and winking, Ellen said, "Oh, no trouble at all. I'll get you both some coffee and get the Spinuccis to fix you a plate." From the back, Mac could hear pots and pans clattering along with a mixture of Italian jibberish. Suddenly, there was a loud crash followed by ranting in Italian. Mac looked concerned.

"Oh, don't worry about them. They're fine." As the noise continued Grace said, "They're like this all the time, yelling at each other. That's how they make love."

"Really? Valentine's day must be a combat zone around here."

Grace chuckled. "Well, it seems to work for them. They've been married for thirty-five years and have raised four children together. I think at this point they'd probably stay together out of spite."

Ellen brought coffee and lingered. Grace looked at her with a puzzling expression as Ellen smiled. Mac looked at Ellen just as puzzled. Ellen's smile widened and then she turned and left.

"You'll have to excuse my aunt. She's off her medication," Grace said loudly so Ellen could hear. Ellen stuck out her tongue at Grace.

"Really, you're aunt? I never would have guessed that."

"Yeah. My father's baby sister."

Taking a sip, Mac asked, "So, how did you end up in Charity working at a little diner? Did you grow up here?"

Grace looked at her coffee. "No. I moved here about nine years ago to live with Ellen. She's been in Charity for years. She's been living here alone since her husband died in the military. My dad and I needed a fresh start. She sort of took us under her wings." Grace looked at her aunt. "She's been very good to me."

"No mother?" Mac asked.

Grace had a faraway look in her eyes. Mac was amazed to watch the sad eyes narrow slightly and take on a fierce hardening. "No mother," she returned.

Hearing the steel in her voice, Mac knew that was no subject to get into. He let the matter drop and just enjoyed the early morning quiet of the diner, since the noise in the kitchen had ceased. After a few minutes, a tall, thin couple came from the kitchen, each carrying a plate filled with steaming pancakes and bacon. Mac hadn't realized how hungry he was until he saw and then smelled the delicious meal.

"Sal and Loretta, I'd like you to meet Mac McCrae. Mac, Sal and Loretta Spinucci."

"Pleasure," the man said. Then turning to Grace, he added, "Miss Grace, this woman. She's ah drivin' me crazy this morning!"

"Me! You are a fool, old man. Is ah no basil in pancakes. Only kiss of garlic," Loretta said using her hands dramatically.

Mac leaned towards Grace and whispered, "I thought you were kidding about the garlic."

"Never come between the Spinuccis and their garlic," she smiled.

Sal continued. "What do I do to deserve such ornery wife?"

"You try to use ah basil in my pancakes, that is what you do." They both started ranting and raving, half in English and half in Italian.

"All right, you two. You don't want Mac here to think his food is poisoned, do you?" The Spinuccis both gasped at the thought. "Now kiss and make up."

"I will endure my enforced imprisonment with this woman." Sal said as Loretta rolled her eyes. "But first, we must see how Mr. Mac like ah his food."

Everyone watched as Mac cautiously cut a piece of the pancake and lifted it to his lips. The sweetness of the spices along with the tartness of the buttermilk and the "kiss of garlic" hit his taste buds suddenly, bursting in a delicious mix of flavors. Mac chewed and savored as the two cooks waited patiently. Finally he said, "I can say with all honesty that these are the greatest pancakes I've ever eaten."

Sal and Loretta cheered. Then they reached for each other and hugged warmly. "I knew the cinnamon was ah your best idea, Sal," Loretta said.

"Oh, no, amore mio, the cinnamon was ah your idea," Sal replied.

Before they could get into another
argument, Grace said, "Well, you're both to be
congratulated. You're the best day cooks in the
universe. Bar none."

The cooks both had huge smiles on their
faces. It brightened the looks of the couple,
changing them from disgruntled senior citizens
to young, happy employees. "Thank you, Miss
Grace," Sal said humbly and taking the hand of
his wife, hurried back to the kitchen.

Mac and Grace smiled at each other and
then dug into their meals. Between bites Mac
asked, "Have Sal and Loretta worked here long?"

"As long as I've been here. I think they
came with the place."

"Does the owner know what a gold mine
he has with them? This food is incredible."

"I think the owner is pleased enough."
Grace avoided looking at Mac.

"I'd like to talk to him."

This brought Grace's attention back up to
Mac. "What?"

"I'd like to talk to the owner."
Unbeknownst to Mac, Ellen's ears had perked up
at this. She stopped her work at the counter and
watched the scene unfold. Sal and Loretta, too,
had heard the request and were listening
intently.

"Why?" Grace asked, taking another bite
of pancake.

"Because I think it is a travesty of justice
that Hal's Place isn't decorated for Christmas. It
brings down the whole look of the town. It's a

black mark on an otherwise beautiful painting. And all because some idiot decides he doesn't like Christmas? What's the matter with this person? I don't know why you all don't demand the curmudgeon put up a few ornaments. What's it gonna hurt?"

A gasp could be heard from the kitchen. The cash register dinked as it was closed. Sensing the coming storm, Ellen and the Spinucci's both made excuses and ducked out the back door. Mac looked back at Grace to see her eyes in that same narrow and fierce expression he had seen previously at the mention of her mother. Only this time, the look was directed at him.

Slowly and deliberately, Grace started speaking. "You're looking at the owner." Mac almost swallowed his tongue. "I'd appreciate not being called an idiot. Curmudgeon I can live with. However, my reasons for not decorating are my own and will not change."

When he could finally find his voice, Mac said, "Sorry. I really didn't mean any harm." Then added, "Care to share why the 'no decorating policy'?"

"No." Then a thought hit Grace. "Why do you even care?"

Be careful here, Mac thought. "Listen, it makes no difference to me, really. I'm just passing through. I was curious. That's all. If it makes you feel better to keep free of any message of goodwill and cheer during the holidays, that's your business."

"I have plenty of goodwill and cheer, every day of the year. It's just Christmas that I'm not too keen about. All this fake happiness. It sets my teeth on edge. A false sense of hope descends on the population and everyone's suppose to fall in line with it, not paying attention to what's really happening in the world. It's like nothing bad could ever happen on Christmas." Grace had started talking to herself at this point. Coming back to the moment, she looked at Mac. "We'll just have to agree to disagree on this point."

"No problem." But there was a big problem. He needed decorations up on Hal's Place. He needed it badly and he needed it quickly. Apparently something terrible had happened to Grace on Christmas so she had decided to remove the whole season from her life. Interesting. Mac wiped his mouth with his napkin and stood to leave. "Well, thanks so much for the breakfast, Grace." His plan was to go back to the hotel room, call his partner, and discuss the problem. Surely, together they could come up with a solution.

"I guess you'll be heading out of town now."

"Nah. I'll hang around for a few more days."

Grace was concerned. She stood and gently touched his shoulder. "Do you have a place to stay?"

Mac was baffled. One moment Grace was shooting arrows with her eyes and the next she was concerned about his welfare. The edges of his lips lifted slightly and he said, "Yeah, sure. I've got a room at the hotel down the street."

"Oh. Good." There didn't seem to be anything left to say. Awkwardly, Grace walked Mac back to the front of the store. She was still concerned about his financial situation. She wasn't sure why. "Listen. I don't know if you're interested in earning a few bucks, but our regular helper is out for a few weeks."

"Helper?"

"Well, specifically our dishwasher and busser. I know it's not glamorous work, but at least it will put a few dollars in your pocket. What do you say?" Grace wasn't sure why it seemed so important to help this man. It only seemed like the right thing to do.

Mac mulled this over. She was offering him a minimum wage job as a busboy. How amazing! Then it hit him—the offer of cake the night before, the offer of water this morning, the breakfast. She thought he was a derelict. How wonderful! Well, turnabout was fair play. She hadn't told him that she was the owner of Hal's so he didn't need to share with her who or what he was.

Trying to get his face to look just eager enough, he said, "That's one of the nicest things I've ever heard of. Thank you. I'd like that." He'd also like to have the opportunity to convince the young woman that she could put up Christmas decorations for this year.

Shaking her hand, Mac said, "When do I start?"

What he was really thinking was *game on!*

CHAPTER THREE

"You did what?" The incredulity in Mac's partner's voice made him laugh out loud.

"I know. Me. Stuart McCrae, photographer extraordinaire is now a busboy."

"Could you enlighten me? I still don't think I understand."

"It's like this, Paula. This town is amazing, a photographer's dream. The main street is decorated to perfection. It's a masterpiece. The only problem is that smack dab in the middle of the picture is this dinky little diner. It's really a perfect setting for it, but the owner won't put up any decorations."

"Why not?"

"She doesn't celebrate Christmas. Or any holiday this time of year. Something happened in her past that made her hate all the whoopla. I took the busboy job because I figure if I can hang around for a while I can talk her into the decorations that I need. In fact, I'm heading there after I talk to you."

"Wait a minute. She?"

"Didn't I mention that before?"

"No, as a matter of fact you didn't." Paula was silent for a beat and then asked, "Just answer me this one question. Is she pretty?"

Mac chuckled. "Why, sweetheart? Are you jealous?"

To that Paula laughed loudly. "No darlin'. They'd put me in jail if I tried to seduce a kid like you."

Mac had always enjoyed his assistant turned partner. The playful banter was just part of how they dealt with each other. Paula was much older than he was but still a beauty. It had been her wisdom and street smarts that had taken McCrae Photography from a local sensation to worldwide recognition. Mac didn't know what he would do without her. He respected her and loved her as a dear friend. She felt the same way about him.

"I just know you and a pretty face. You've got to get that last picture for the new book in the next few weeks. Now's not the time to lose all objectivity. Which reminds me. Did you get the money I wired you?" Paula said with a hint of "I told you so" in her voice.

"Yeah, I got it. Thanks."

"Why didn't you call your folks?"

Mac sighed. "I'm not sure where they are at the moment. Somewhere in Africa, I think. Besides I didn't want to track them down only to receive a lecture from them." Then sensing Paula opening her mouth he added, "And don't you start."

Paula chuckled. Any girl seriously interested in Mac would have to come through her first. She'd make sure of it. "Hey, do you want me to come up? I mean, now that your *assistant* isn't there."

"Very funny. I think I'd like to use someone from around here. I've already gotten some great shots but there might one better out there just waiting for me. I need someone who knows the area."

"Gotcha. Just let me know if you need me."

Mac clicked off his phone and thought about what Paula had asked. Was Grace pretty? Yes, she was very attractive. She was slender, maybe a little too slender, and she carried herself with an air of confidence. It made sense to Mac now that she was a business owner. Her laugh was melodious—like an orchestra playing a spring concert. Her kindness showed a loveliness that came from within. But those eyes. They expressed just what she was feeling. Most of the time, that emotion seemed to be a deep sadness.

Mac shook himself. He was here for a picture. That was all. Grace meant nothing to him but a way of reaching his goal. He looked down at his opened suitcase. He let out a rough breath. If he could just get this last picture for his book *Christmas In America*, he'd fulfill his contract with his publisher. Then he could stop this infernal traveling and settle down in the warm climate of Miami Beach and lay on the sand, watching girls in bikinis go by.

The thought made him more determined than ever to finish the project. He changed into his oldest tee shirt and brushed his teeth. Looking into the mirror, Mac said, "Okay McCrae. Go figure out how to get the damn picture."

Afternoons were slow at the diner. That is until about three thirty. Every school day at that time, the kids of the town loved to descend on Hal's Diner for a milkshake or ice cream sundae or just a piece of penny candy. It brightened Grace's day to see the children. Even though it got chaotic at times, she loved it.

Mac looked in from the kitchen to see kids everywhere. Every seat at the counter was taken with Ellen making ice cream dishes as fast as she could, a smile on her face.

Grace was at the front of the store where the penny candy waited for eager young buyers. She made them get in an orderly line so she could help them one at a time. Mac walked to the front counter and said to Grace, "Need any help?"

Turning to see him, Grace's face was flush and her eyes were . . . happy. Mac was mesmerized. He couldn't have spoken if his life depended on it.

"No, I'm good. Let me introduce you." Then to Mac's surprise, Grace stuck two fingers in her mouth and let out an ear-piercing whistle. All the children in the store immediately quieted down and looked at her. "Kids, I'd like to introduce someone to you. This is Mac McCrae. Mac'll be taking Jimmy's place while his broken leg is healing."

"Broken leg?" This was the first that Mac had heard about the former busboy.

"He fell off his shoes," Grace explained.

"What?"

"The annual decorating of the town last Friday night. Jimmy was dressed in costume as a candy cane. His shoes were the high stilts. He didn't see an ornament that had rolled into the street and he fell and broke his leg."

"Okay, I guess that sounds reasonable." This was certainly an interesting town, Mac thought.

All the kids looked at him. Some said, "Hi." Others smiled or waved. A group of tween-aged girls giggled and stared at him. Mac winked at them, sending them out the door squealing.

"Hey! You're scaring the customers," Grace said good-naturedly. She knew exactly how the girls felt. A look from Mac would send any female swooning.

"Sorry." He took a moment to look at the children in the room. He would love to find a responsible boy to help him set up shots around the town and be his gofer. Maybe he could get a few suggestions from Grace. But then he'd have to tell her why he needed an assistant. It could get complicated.

"Merry Christmas, Mr. Mac."

Mac looked down to see an adorable little girl with bright blue eyes and two blonde ponytails staring back at him. Unable to resist, he knelt down to get eye-to-eye with her. "Merry Christmas to you, honey. What's your name?"

"I'm Holly. Me and Miss Grace are good friends."

He chuckled. "I'm glad. What you got there?" Mac asked pointing to the candy in her hands.

"It's a peppermint. One for me and one for my mama. It's the only Christmas candy Miss Grace has."

Mac whispered in her ear. "That's a real shame, isn't it? I think that's something we need to work on, don't you?"

Little Holly giggled at him as the door opened and a young boy about fifteen came in the door. "Holly," he called.

"That's my brother Noel. I'd better go. Bye, Mr. Mac."

With a big smile just for Holly, Mac said, "See you later, Holly." He watched the small girl walk to her brother. Noel put his arm around her and led her through the front door. *Hmmm*, Mac thought. Maybe this Noel would make a good assistant for him.

After one last look at the brother and sister, Mac turned back to watch Grace handing out wrapped candy with one hand and taking money with the other. And then the thought hit him. It was so brilliant; Mac didn't know why he hadn't thought of it before.

The children.

They were the answer to his problem. Christmas and children go together. Grace loved the children. Ergo, all he had to do was get Grace to understand the need for Hal's Place to cater to the needs of the children. After all, like Holly said, they didn't even have any Christmas candy.

Yeah, that's the ticket. It's for the children. Who could resist that?

Sensing that Grace could use some help, Mac jumped in and helped with serving the pint-sized customers. When everyone had been helped, Mac turned to Grace. She was closing the register and making some notes about her stock.

"You know, little Holly was disappointed that you only had peppermint for Christmas candy. Aren't you worried about disappointing the kids by not celebrating Christmas?"

"No," Grace said casually. "The kids love me anyway. I'm the lady that sells them penny candy."

Mac snickered. "That must endear you to their parents."

"Well, not the parents, but definitely their dentists." Then looking up at Mac she said solemnly, "I don't think a little bit of sweetness in a child's life is going to hurt them."

"Just not Christmas. It doesn't bother you that there are no reminders, no celebration of the most important holiday of the year here at Hal's? I mean, for the children?"

And as she walked towards her office she said, "You keep Christmas in your way and I'll keep it in mine."

When the office door closed, Mac muttered, "Spoken like a true Scrooge."

Ellen saw to the needs of the last child in the store. Then as things had quieted down, she chose a booth to sit in and put her feet up. Grace brought out two cups of coffee and sat down across from her.

"Whew! All those kids are a handful. I think I'm getting too old to handle them," Ellen said.

"Never!" Grace grinned as she sipped her coffee.

Ellen carefully stirred her coffee and in a low voice said, "That Mac fellow seems nice."

"Yeah. I guess."

Looking at him working through the kitchen pass-through she added, "Good looking fellow. Real sweet to the kids."

Grace knew what her aunt was doing. Ellen was so afraid that Grace would end up alone. Considering all that she had been through, Grace didn't really think that a bad thing. "Don't go there, Ellen."

Innocently, Ellen looked at her. "Why Grace, whatever do you mean?"

Sorry to burst Ellen's bubble, Grace said, "He's a drifter."

"A what?"

"You know, a guy that just goes from town to town, picking up a job here and there, no roots."

"Are you sure?"

Leaning over, Grace whispered, "I found him on a bench, the other side of the lake yesterday morning. I figured he spent the night there. He has no money, old clothes, travels on a motorcycle. I think when you add all that up, you get drifter."

Ellen looked back at Mac, hard at work. "Oh, that's a shame. He really has nice eyes."

"And a nice smile," Grace said before she could stop herself. Then wanting to change the subject, she said, "Hey, I almost forgot. Have you heard from Howard?"

A look of disapproval appeared on Ellen's face. "Yes." She sipped her hot coffee.

When her aunt didn't say anything, Grace said, "Well?"

"He called me last night, when I got home from work. We . . . had words."

"You two argued? Whatever about?" Grace couldn't believe it. Ellen was the most docile person she knew. And Mayor Scott was known for his likeability, his ease around people.

Ellen hesitated. She loved her niece dearly but she wasn't sure that she wanted to share this with her. But she knew Grace. Grace was a mother hen for those she loved. Ellen knew that Grace wouldn't let up until she had the whole story. She swallowed hard and said, "Howard wants . . . he wants . . ."

"For God's sake, Ellen spit it out! I'm on pins and needles here."

"Okay. He wants to date me exclusively! There, are you happy?" Ellen was flustered. Looking down, she nervously rubbed her coffee cup.

Grace's face brightened. Ellen had been alone for too long. This should have been good news. She wasn't sure why it wasn't. Quietly, she asked, "And that's not a good thing?"

When Ellen looked up she had tears in her eyes. "I just don't know if I can. It's been so long, Grace. I've forgotten how to care for a man."

Her heart went out to Ellen. Grace had lost much in life but she couldn't begin to understand how it felt to lose your spouse, your partner, your soul mate. Grace reached over and took Ellen's hand. "How do you feel about Howard, Ellen?"

Thinking about it for a moment, Ellen then said, "He's a great guy. He's kind, understanding, easy to talk to. He's just great."

Something wasn't right here. "Okay, he's great. But how do you *feel* about him? Any sparks? Any heat?"

Ellen's face turned red. "Grace, we shouldn't be talking about these kinds of things."

That old Southern way of life. It was endearing and at times frustrating. "I'm family, Ellen. Tell me. It might help you." And it might help Grace know if she should have a talk with the mayor about her aunt.

Sighing Ellen said, "When Bill died, I thought that part of my life was over for good. Then Howard held my hand. It was like holding on to a live wire. It feels so good to just feel again."

Grace smiled. "Then there's the answer. It *is* a good thing."

Ellen jumped up and took her coffee cup to the dirty dish bin. "I'm not sure it is. What do I know about dating and men and . . . things? It's just been too long."

"Nonsense," Grace said following her. "Howard's a nice guy. There's attraction. Nothing wrong with seeing where this relationship is going?"

"But Grace—"

"When are you seeing him again?"

Ellen looked around to see what she could do. She grabbed a rag and began cleaning the counter. Looking intently at her work she mumbled, "I told him I'd have to get back to him."

Not willing to let this slide, Grace walked to the office and reached into Ellen's purse, pulling out her cell phone. She marched back to Ellen and shoved the phone in her face. "Call him."

Ellen's breath started coming quickly. "What do I say?"

"Tell him you'd love to see him again." When Ellen just looked at the phone, Grace said softly, "Ellen, really, don't let this chance slip by. Do you know how hard it is to find a nice, available guy over twenty-one and under eighty-one in Charity?" Ellen still hesitated. Grace encouraged her by saying, "Come on. You'll thank me later."

Ellen slowly took the phone and punched in the number. When she asked to speak to Howard, she looked up at Grace, fear in her eyes. Grace smiled tenderly at her and touched her arm.

"Hello, Howard? It's Ellen Charles. Is this a bad time?" The answer obviously was to Ellen's liking because a smile crept on her face.

"Good. Hold on just for a second." She covered the phone and said to Grace, "I'm going to take this in the office."

Grace couldn't help chuckling as Ellen almost ran for the privacy of the office. "Good thinking."

Mac's schedule was flexible. Grace had told him that she would take any hours that he could give. He only had to clock in and out. With that freedom, Mac decided to take a few hours off after the invasion of the school kids. He went back to his hotel room and grabbed his camera.

The weather was a perfect Chamber of Commerce day. The sky was a bright blue with a scattering of puffy clouds and the temperature was a comfortable seventy-five. No need for a jacket now. Which was good and bad—no hiding his camera. Mac hated the thought of people seeing the camera and instantly tensing up.

He walked back and forth along the pretty tree-lined streets of Charity. Town ordinances insisted that yards and house exteriors were kept tidy. It made for a pretty little town that would delight any photographer. Mac was having a ball with his camera. He found an older man standing on a ladder putting up Christmas lights on his house. The next street over, a teenage boy wearing a Santa cap was washing his car. Probably getting ready to pick up his girl for a spin. He saw a group of children playing in a little park, their faces bright with the excitement of the day. The whole town just seemed to make him happy. He frowned. Did the residents of Charity put some kind of spell on those visiting?

He forced his mind back to Miami Beach. Yeah, warm beach days and sultry, romantic nights. That was more his style.

Turning the corner, Mac saw a young boy in the yard of a modest, one-story home. He was raking stray leaves with an intense look on his face. Mac recognized him as Holly's brother. He quickly walked over. "Noel." The boy looked up. "It's Noel, right?"

"Yes sir." The boy was cautious of the stranger. Mac couldn't blame him.

Holding out his hand for Noel to shake it, Mac said, "Hi, I'm Mac McCrae. I work for Grace Hudson at Hal's Place."

Noel took the hand, feeling good that the man wasn't treating him as a kid. "Yes sir?"

"I met your sister Holly, today. I guess you came in to bring her home."

"Yes sir." Noel didn't know what else to say.

Mac smiled at him. "You can call me Mac. Listen, I've got an offer to make to you. Is your mom or dad at home?"

"Yes sir." When Mac lifted his eyebrows, Noel added, "Yeah, my dad is."

"Great." Then slapping a hand on Noel's shoulder, he led him to the front porch. "Let's have a little talk with him."

The talk went well. Noel's father had been impressed when he realized who Mac was. Secrecy was asked of the family. Although Holly still wasn't sure what the big deal was, she agreed to keep the secret. She just plain liked Mac and felt comfortable enough to sit by him while Mac made his offer to have Noel's assistance.

Walking back into the diner, Mac was whistling, pleased with himself. He clocked back in, donned an apron, and grabbed a bin and washcloth. A big burly man stood in the kitchen chopping onions and tomatoes. Mac said, "Hey." Without looking up, the man raised the knife in greeting and continued his work.

Looking into the dining area, he saw only a few people scattered about enjoying a cup of coffee as they worked on their laptops or talked with others. Ellen was standing behind the counter reading the paper.

"Hey. What are you still doing here?" he said, surprising Ellen.

"Grace had to go see a supplier. There was a little mix-up on an order so she went to straighten it out."

"Oh." Mac motioned towards the kitchen with his head. "Who's the big guy in the kitchen with the sharp knife?"

Ellen snickered. "That's Bruiser, our prep guy and relief cook. He usually comes in the afternoon to help out. Tom's coming in a little late so Bruiser's on for him until then."

"Scary. Anything you'd like me to do?"

"Yeah," Ellen said putting down her newspaper. "Grab a stool and let me pour you a cup of coffee."

Mac smiled and put down his bin and rag. He sat in front of Ellen as she poured. "It sure is nice today but I hear there's another cold front coming in soon."

"Yeah, that's the thing about Central Florida winters. It may get cold. Real cold. But it's only for a few days. Then it's back to paradise. So, you're from Miami Beach, I hear."

Oh. Mac was wondering when the inquisition would come. Well, better get it over with. "That's right. Born and raised there. I love it."

"Why are you here?" Ellen said with a little heat.

"Wow. You certainly get to the point. I guess you could say I'm traveling around, seeing part of the country."

Ellen nodded her head. "I see. So you're just passing through." It wasn't a question.

"That's right. Is something wrong?"

"No. Nothing." Ellen hesitated. "Really nothing." Mac waited. "It's just that you're a good looking guy. You seem to be nice; a hard worker."

When Ellen didn't elaborate, Mac said, "Ohhhkay."

Then Ellen looked him straight in the eyes and said, "Grace has been alone for a while now. She hasn't dated in the past two years that I know of. I don't want to see her hurt."

Mac was taken aback. He truly didn't know what to say. He found Grace extremely attractive—great body, nice face. He wouldn't mind a little affection while he was in town but considering things, it would complicate everything if he were to get involved with Grace. "Ellen, I'm here for a short time. I may even leave before Christmas." If he had his way about it. "Grace has been very kind to me. I wouldn't hurt her."

Without missing a beat, Ellen replied, "What's the matter? Don't you think she's pretty?"

Totally confused, Mac replied, "She's gorgeous! I thought you just said—"

"A man couldn't do better than my niece. She's got a good heart. If she could just get over this Christmas thing, but I don't see that happening since she . . ."

"What?" Mac's curiosity was peaked.

Ellen smiled sadly. "Never mind. You better drink that coffee before it gets cold."

Mac tasted the hot liquid, the best he'd ever tasted. "If there's any way I can help her with this Christmas phobia, I'd like to, Ellen."

Pausing, Ellen chose her words carefully. "It's not exactly a phobia. She just had a very hard Christmas a while back and can't seem to get over it."

"All the more reason to help her." Here was his opening, Mac thought. After all, he had a kindred spirit in Ellen. "Why don't I go over to the super mart and pick up some decorations.

We'll put them up and Grace will love it so much
that she'll forget all about this silly Christmas
hatred."

"If it was only that easy." Ellen drank her
coffee and sighed heavily. "I keep thinking if
only Hal had handled things differently."

"Hal? As in Hal's Diner? What's he got to
do with this?" Mac was getting confused again.
Ellen had a way of jumping from one train of
thought to another without telling anyone which
train to take.

Ellen had gone deep in her thoughts.
Turning back to Mac she said, "Hal, my brother,
Grace's father."

"Really?" The plot thickens. "Well, I'd
love to meet the elusive Hal. What, did he dump
all this on Grace and decide to retire to the
tropics or something?"

"Or something." Ellen's sad eyes looked
into Mac's. "He died two years ago."

"Oh. I'm so sorry." Mac placed his hand
softly over Ellen's.

The compassion was not unnoticed by
Ellen. "Thank you, Mac."

Mac tightened his grip on Ellen's hand.
"Tell me. What happened?"

After pausing to take a breath, Ellen
began. "Hal didn't . . . take care of himself. He
worked all the time. Wouldn't let me or Grace do
much of anything. I basically stayed by the cash
register. Grace kept the financial books. That
was all. He got real sick with a cold and a cough

that turned into pneumonia. By the time we finally got him to the hospital, it was too late."

Ellen dapped a napkin to her eyes. "He left the diner to Grace and me. I didn't want it, so I signed my half over to her. Ever since then she's been trying to sell it and move to New York City to be an accountant. That's what she trained for in college. She wants to move, to leave all the memories behind."

Mac hadn't meant to bring back such hard memories for Ellen. He began to rub the hand that he held between both of his. "Is that why Grace hates Christmas?"

"That's just part of it."

"What's the rest?"

Looking into the caring blue eyes of Mac, Ellen thought she would love to tell him the whole story, but she couldn't. "It's not for me to tell." Then she smiled at him and with her free hand, patted his cheek. "You're a good guy, Mac. I'm glad you're here, even if it's only for a short time."

"Thanks. So, how about that run to the super mart for decorations?"

Ellen couldn't help it. She sincerely liked this young man. Grinning at him she said, "You keep that thought. But we'll need to work a little more subtly on Grace. I don't think she's quite ready for jingle bells, do you?"

Mac reluctantly shook his head. "You're probably right. Just leave it to me. I've got a few ideas. Before you know it, she'll be singing

Christmas carols like a reformed Scrooge on Christmas morning."

"God bless us everyone," Ellen added with a hopeful grin.

CHAPTER FOUR

His plan set, Mac began implementation. He already had an ally in Ellen. Cross that off his list. One evening when Grace wasn't there, he moved the decorations he had purchased at the super mart from his hotel room to the storeroom. Check. He carried on casual conversations with the cooks—Tom, Sal and Loretta, Bruiser—to enlist their help in transforming Hal's Place. All were avid Christmas lovers. Double check.

Talking to Bruiser had been fun, Mac thought sarcastically. The man barely said more than two words at one time. He was a good worker, though, who appreciated good workers around him. Mac helped him slice apples and peel potatoes, a skill that Mac's beloved grandmother had pushed him to learn. Bruiser appreciated the help and Mac found that if he helped the large man, Bruiser would actually say a few words to him.

Mac found that all the cooks were sad that Grace didn't celebrate the season. They all had the holiday off, except for Grace who insisted on working. Her reason was that she wanted to be there in case anyone needed nourishment. No one bought that reason.

Mac's plan began with subtle ideas before progressing to the below the belt, straight to the gut ideas.

One day he casually said to Grace, "Can I leave some stuff out front?" Mac had intentionally waited until Grace was counting the noon receipts to ask her. He knew that after filling out a deposit slip and putting the money in a leather bag, she'd go into the office, grab her purse and coat, and leave. That would give him time to really decorate the place. Then he could run back to his room for his camera. As soon as the lights in the town came on, he'd run outside, get his picture, and then head for the palm trees of Miami Beach before dawn's first light. He was giddy with the thought.

"Fifty-six, fifty-seven, yeah whatever, fifty-eight . . ."

Mac smiled smugly and carried several bags out the front door. The wind had started, bringing in colder weather. Mac pulled his jacket closer to him and wished he had gloves. Who wears gloves in Florida? he thought.

His eyes as wide as his grin, he looked into the bags to see his Christmas treasures. There were two wreaths to put on the front door and the emergency door. There were small multi-colored lights for the small bushes in front of the building. Big bright red bows would hang above every other window. Battery operated candles would be put inside, at every window. And of course lots of large multi-colored lights outlining the building.

Mac pulled out a few strings of the smaller Christmas lights. A warm feeling came over him as he remembered putting up lights with his grandmother. He gently began layering the lights across and through the bushes as he remembered how she had been adamant about decorating their large house. She wanted it to be a big display but said it should be "elegant without venturing over into the realm of tacky." Mac chuckled as he remembered that they had never been able to pull that off. It had been tacky.

And he had loved it.

When he got his own house in Miami Beach, he was going to make sure that it was a showplace at Christmas. Lots of lights, lots of music, lots of love. Just like his grandmother would have wanted.

Humming "Joy to the World" Mac continued to string the bushes. Yes sir, as soon as Christmas was over, he was going to be looking for a house. His own house that he could finally settle down in. Too bad he didn't have someone to share it with him but that was okay for now. The right girl would come across his path one day. He thought, *all I have to do is be patient. Not settle for less than what I want. I can wait. After all I'm only—*

A steady tapping noise caught his attention and he looked over to see Grace standing on the top step, arms crossed, impatiently tapping her foot. The sight of her with fire in her eyes, serious expression, and ramrod straight posture was so becoming that it almost made him forget that he was in serious trouble.

"Hi," he sheepishly said.

"What do you think you're doing?" Her voice was low, ominous even.

Mac racked his brain for a suitable response. "I found these lights in the bushes. I knew you wouldn't like them there, so I was getting them out for you." At Grace's one raised eyebrow Mac tried again. "Okay, it's like this. I thought it was going to freeze tonight, so I'm using this line to anchor a sheet . . . that . . . I'll . . . get." Grace narrowed her eyes, dropped her arms, and fisted her hands at her sides. For some reason, Mac couldn't help digging his grave a little deeper. "How about this one. I was just standing here and the wind blew these lights over just as you were coming out the front door." He looked expectantly at her.

Grace walked over to Mac. He stood to face her. Although he was taller than her by about six inches, her posture showed her dominance at the moment. In a deadly menacing voice Grace said, "Perhaps I didn't make myself clear. Let me try again. Hal's Place will not be decorated with 'found' lights, lights to hold down sheets, or wind-blown lights. There will be no decorations on the building. Is that so hard to understand?"

"Yes, it is," Mac sincerely said. "Why not, Grace?"

She backed up and quickly said between clinched teeth, "It's none of your business. Now, remove these things at once. I'm going to make a deposit at the bank and then I'll be back. If everything is not removed, I'm calling the sheriff's office. Are we clear?"

Mac frowned at her. "Yeah. Crystal."

The nerve of that man! Grace stomped her way to the bank thinking about what had just happened. She had rules. They were her rules and it was her diner. So there.

Then she thought about Mac. She thought about the way the wind blew his black hair in his face as his eyes looked hopefully at her—all the while he was coming up with excuses for the lights. Ridiculous excuses at that. Did he really think she'd believe that the wind blew lights into her bushes?

Suddenly, the absurdity of the situation hit her, and she couldn't help it. She burst out laughing—not an easy laugh, but a deep, loud guffaw. The sound was foreign to her. But it felt so good. A knot of tension she didn't even know she was carrying loosened as the laughter continued.

Mac was something else. She would have to keep her eyes on him.

Okay, the "suddenly decorated, how in the world did that happen?" route didn't work. Time to try something else. A few days later, Mac showed up with a file folder and a couple of large posters.

Grace was curious but was quickly distracted with the busy morning. She hadn't said two words to Mac since the confrontation over the lights. She didn't dare. Yes, she was still a bit mad at him but she couldn't forget the laughter. After returning from the bank that day, she found she couldn't look at him without a giggle catching in her throat.

She had been thinking a lot about Mac. He was handsome, funny, kind, likeable. And that smile. At the thought of it, Grace could feel herself getting weak. Given the right circumstances, she could see herself falling for the guy. But facts were facts. He was a drifter, just passing through town. With an awfully strong desire to decorate her business. *That's right, Grace. Hold on to that anger. Otherwise . . .* Grace didn't want to think of otherwise.

The substitute waitress that they sometimes used, Sally, had been called in to help for the holidays. The young redhead was busy cleaning up after the morning rush as Grace slipped into her office to do some paperwork. Mac found her there leaning over her calculator, crunching numbers with the speed and efficiency of a Fortune five hundred CEO.

Sensing the presence of another person and without looking up Grace murmured, "Can I help you?"

"Yeah." Mac entered the small office, closing the door and sitting in a folding chair in front of the desk. He glanced around and noticed that everything was in its place. The calendar on the wall was on the correct month. The pencils were in their own mug, sharpened to a point and ready to go. The file cabinet was next to the desk, closed, dusted, and cleared on the top. The desk contained a basket with a few file folders in it. A computer was on a side table, and in front of Grace was her large calculator along with a thick ledger that Grace was writing in when not punching the calculator.

Mac cringed thinking of his own office. The top of his desk was always cluttered with photos and proof sheets. No calculator in sight. There would be several Styrofoam cups of coffee—hopefully Paula had thought to look in and throw them away. And did he remember to get rid of the lunch from KFC before he left? He shuddered to think it might still be there.

When Mac didn't say anything, Grace looked up. "What?"

"I should have figured that your office would look like this. I mean you're always here. Don't you have a life outside of the diner?"

"Your concern about my lonely existence has been dully noted. Now, if there isn't anything else, I've got work to do." And she bent her head to get back to it.

Mac casually said, "Well, if you're not interested in how you could finally sell this place then I'll just wander back into the kitchen." He started to stand.

"No, wait!" Mac sat back down with a smug smile. "Do you know of someone that might like to buy the diner?"

"I know a way to sell it," he corrected.

Grace turned off her calculator, sat back, and folded her arms. "Okay. Let's hear it."

"It all has to do with packaging. You've got to make this business irresistible for potential buyers."

"Agreed. How do I do that?"

Just what he wanted to hear. "By brightening it up. Just look around you. There's no happiness, no joy, no . . . love."

"What?"

"Really. You don't want to sell a restaurant. People don't want to buy just a restaurant. They want to buy happiness, joy, and love."

Grace didn't trust him. "Uh-huh. And just how do I showcase these qualities, marketing whiz that you are?"

Ignoring her sarcasm, Mac put a file folder on her desk but kept his hand on top of it. "Companies all over the world work hard to succeed in business and no matter what they do or try, they notice that their companies always experience a drastic upturn in December. Do you know why?"

"No. Tell me." Grace didn't like where this was going.

"It's the holiday season, and before you cut me off . . ." Mac lifted his hand seeing that Grace was already opening her mouth to protest. "The vast majority of the world's population is in a good mood during this month. They're happy to part with their money, invest their dollars. It's a perfect time for a new venture. A charming restaurant in an adorable little Florida town would hold lots of promise for any entrepreneur if they could look at the property and feel that good mood."

Grace narrowed her eyes at Mac. "And they can't right now?"

"No. The outside of this diner looks like a relic from the 1950's. Which is nice," Mac hastened to add when Grace began to interrupt. "It fits the nostalgic feel of the town. However, at this time of year that good mood can only come with a beautiful display of . . ."

Mac picked up the poster and showed it to her. "Tada! Christmas!" At the top of the poster was the word "Christmas" in carefully scripted ink. All around the poster were pictures of the town of Charity. The pictures where of businesses and homes tastefully decorated for the season, with pictures of the undecorated Hal's place interspersed. In the middle of the poster was a graph drawn in red and green inks. There were figures on the graph demonstrating that for the last five years, more businesses were sold in December than any other month of the year. Quotes from buyers were included in little bubbles saying things like "I couldn't resist the Christmas lights" and "I felt the true meaning of the season and had to buy it."

"I have more figures and facts in the folder," Mac said as he gestured at the folder on her desk.

Grace couldn't believe her eyes. "How did you do all this?"

Remembering that he was supposed to be down on his luck, not carrying around an expensive laptop, he said, "Charity's got a great library." Not a lie. He supposed that the town really did have a good library.

"Also to sweeten the pot," Mac pulled out another poster. "This graph will show you the statistics for businesses that decorate for Christmas versus those that don't. The diner could pick up thirty percent more profits with a little garland and tinsel."

Opening the folder, Grace looked over the different information Mac had provided for her. The accountant in her was very impressed. It was a very good presentation. Thoughtful. Insightful. Smart. It didn't jive with her view of a drifter.

Her eyes went back to the pictures on the poster. "Where did you get these pictures?"

"Oh, those?" Maybe the pictures had gone over the top, but he couldn't help think that they showed the sharp contrast between Hal's and the rest of the town. "I . . . took them."

Grace stood and reached for the poster. Looking closely at the photos she said, "They're very good." After a minute of admiring them, she added, "Have you ever thought about selling your pictures? They're excellent."

Mac wanted to laugh but bit his tongue instead. "Thanks. But you're missing the point. A great way to showcase Hal's *and* bring in more business, which is also very enticing to buyers, is to put up Christmas decorations."

Grace didn't say anything as she looked up at Mac.

Not sure what she was thinking, Mac said, "You won't have to do anything. I'll do it all. Just say the word."

After a moment of silence, Grace handed the poster back to Mac. She sat down and turned her calculator back on. She looked back at her work and before punching in numbers, said, "No."

"No?"

"No," she returned without looking at him.

Mac dropped the posters. He stood up and placing his palms on the desk leaned over so that he was directly in her line of vision. "What about presenting happiness, joy, love, brightening up the place?"

Defiantly she looked into his eyes. "Excellent idea. We'll paint." Then as she proceeded to punch in numbers she said, "maybe even get a few pictures to hang on the wall."

Dejected, Mac picked up the posters. He mumbled, "You need professional photographs, not pictures." Grace didn't reply. He laid the posters on the folding chair. "I'll leave these visuals here with you whenever you have time to study them." Grace still didn't reply. As he closed the door to return to the kitchen he thought, *round two over.*

Grace studied the numbers in her ledger but didn't really see them. A vision of Mac kept swimming in front of her eyes. The zealousness of his presentation, the imaginative posters he had worked on, the excitement of his voice all jumbled together to make working impossible.

Then a giggle escaped her lips before she could smother it with her hands. He was so cute. His perseverance was admirable. She had wanted so much to give him a big smile. To reach for him, to run her fingers through his unruly hair. To kiss his cheek. Maybe, kiss his chin, his neck, his lips. *Stop it*! She told herself. Not happening. She rubbed her hands over her face. What she needed was a short walk to help clear her head.

As she put on her jacket to leave, she looked again at the pictures on the poster. They were excellent. There was a style to them that looked so familiar to her. She couldn't put her finger on it. Shrugging, she walked out of the office and the diner and into the brisk cold to get her senses back before the onslaught of the lunch crowd. As she walked she found herself thinking, *I wonder what Mac's next scheme will be?*

Mac had managed to slip away right before dusk. He had some tricky shots lined up and was meeting Noel in the lobby of the hotel to start. For these pictures, a tripod was needed, as were filters and a variety of lenses. He had purposely chosen an out of the way place to shoot where no one from the diner would see him and report back to Grace. He was so enjoying playing the part of a nobody. The anonymity was fun.

On a quiet edge of the jogging trail around the lake, Mac set up his equipment. "Set the tripod up on the backside of the trail"

Noel went to work, eager to do a good job. He was a quiet young man that seemed to hold a lot of thoughts inside of him. Mac wondered if that was healthy, so he tried to get him to talk.

"So, Noel. How long have you lived in Charity?"

"Ah, a little over six months, I guess," Noel mumbled.

"Do you like it?"

"It's okay."

They worked in silence. Mac began snapping pictures of a cozy little town as the darkness of night began to descend upon it. The Christmas lights would be turned on any minute, a dusting of jewels in the increasing shadows.

As Noel handed Mac a wipe to clear the condensation off the lens, Mac started his conversation again. "Are you excited about Christmas?"

"Nah."

Mac looked at him. This sounded too much like a certain diner owner with sad eyes. "Why not?"

Noel sighed. "What's there to be excited about? It's just another day. There's still wars going on. There's still people starving in the world. People still hurt each other and . . ." Noel shrugged and reached his hand out for the used wipe that Mac was holding. "There's nothing I can do about any of it. Celebrating Christmas won't change anything."

Noel's short speech amazed Mac. *There's more here than meets the eye.* He handed the wipe to Noel and then continued to adjust the view of his camera. "You know what? You're right. Nothing, not even Christmas, is going to stop the world from continuing on." Without looking up, Mac continued to tweak the camera lens. "But it's kinda nice to take a moment every year to stop and . . . just be happy. My grandma used to say no matter how bad things were, there was always someone whose situation was worse than mine. She said it helps, especially at this time of year, to help others less fortunate."

Mac looked at Noel from the corner of his eye. No response. His voice now serious, Mac said, "My grandma died this past spring. This is my first Christmas without her. And although it's really sad not to have her with me anymore, I remember how she felt about Christmas."

Noel was looking down. Quietly he asked, "How did she feel about Christmas?"

"She thought it was the best time of the year. It was a time for everyone to put hard feelings aside and think good thoughts. It was time for people to look up into the sky, at the stars and think about the star that shone brightly that first Christmas. And no matter what had happened that year, it was time for 'peace on earth, goodwill to all men.'" Mac glanced at Noel to see him ponder this.

Then as he looked back into the viewfinder, the lights of Charity came on and his breath caught. He started clicking pictures furiously. The beauty of the moment was overwhelming. "And if you let it, Christmas can always bring a little magic." He continued clicking as Noel stared at the lights, thinking.

After replacing the lens with one having a softer focus, Mac said, "I know my grandma is looking down on me and she would skin me alive if I didn't celebrate Christmas in the biggest way possible."

The image of an old woman intimidating Mac brought a laugh to Noel. Thinking of what Mac had just said Noel asked, "How do you do that? I mean celebrate Christmas in the biggest way?"

Mac thought. "By remembering that Christmas is all about a gift. A wonderful gift." Giving a shrug he added, "So I try to give." Noel thought about that. Mac could see the struggle in the boy's face. He put his hand on Noel's shoulder and said, "Giving to others always help me to forget the bad things of life. I realize that I'm not so bad off. I'm thankful for what I've got instead of bitter for what I've lost."

Noel's big eyes looked up at Mac. There was a spark of hope in them. "I bet your grandma is real proud of you," he said to Mac.

Mac's smile was wide. His face glowed. "I like to think so, kid." As he started to put his equipment away, Mac said, "That's enough shots for today. Let's get this stuff back to the hotel and then I'll buy you a hot chocolate, okay?" At Noel's smile and nod, Mac added, "Grace makes the best hot chocolate, you know. That diner has the best everything. Although it could use a touch of Christmas."

Noel laughed. "Good luck with that. I've heard how Miss Grace feels about Christmas."

As they each grabbed a bag of equipment and started walking, Mac said, "Working on it, kid." And he winked at Noel.

The first grade of the Charity Elementary School had arranged to come by the diner at the end of their holiday field trip through the little downtown area. Grace had napkins with two chocolate chip cookies each spread out all over the restaurant. She loved to have the kids come in anytime, and even if she didn't like Christmas, it was heartwarming to see them so excited.

An hour later she wondered if it had been such a good idea. The noise level was through the roof. Sal and Loretta were trying to prepare the lunch special so they weren't much help. Ellen had a luncheon date with Howard that she had to primp for so she wasn't there. Sally couldn't come until noon. Grace had hoped that Mac would have been there but he had shown up before opening to help get everything ready and then took off before the troops had arrived. *Coward!*

Grace hurried through the dining room with a pitcher of milk in one hand and a pitcher of water in the other hand. And a rag tucked into her apron to clean up the spills. Her hair was starting to fall from her ponytail, her feet hurt, and the smile that she had started the day with was fading fast.

The sound of the front door opening and the joyous yells of the children sent Grace jerking around. A man in a Santa suit came strutting in saying, "Ho, ho, ho." Grace couldn't believe her eyes. As the kids tried to crowd "Santa" the teachers gave the students their signal to be quiet. Knowing Santa's observant eyes where on them, they decided to be on their best behavior.

"Well, now. What a nice bunch of boys and girls we have here. Ho, ho, ho. Tell me, kids. Have you been good this year?" The children answered with a deafening "Yes!"

"Ho, ho, ho. That's good. Suppose I sit down and have each one of you come tell me what you want for Christmas and then I'll give you a little treat."

While the kids cheered and the teachers organized, Grace took a minute to study this "Santa." It wasn't hard to figure out. The laughing blue eyes and shining white teeth gave him away. Was this Mac's next ploy to get her to decorate Hal's? Well, it was cute but it wasn't going to change her mind. As she put the pitchers down and began collecting trash, she watched Mac with the children. He was so loving, so gentle, a natural with children. He played his part well. The kids were enjoying this impromptu meeting very much. It had also helped her, giving her a break from the kids and allowing her to start cleaning up. She would try to be nice and thank him later on.

Mac gave each child a wrapped candy cane with instructions to wait until they got home in the afternoon and got their parent's permission to eat it. After each child had had a turn with "Santa," Mac looked at Grace and in a loud voice said, "What about you, little girl?"

CHAPTER FIVE

The room went silent as all eyes turned to Grace who was wiping tables. "Huh?" she croaked out.

"Come on, Miss Grace," the children began to implore.

Her cheeks grew red. How dare Mac put her into this position. He was going to get an earful when the kids left.

Several children took her hands and others pushed her from behind towards the 'jolly, old man.' Grace sneered down at him. Then, remembering the kids, she gave a smile, gritting her teeth.

Mac was amazed he didn't see any fangs.

With narrow, piercing eyes Grace acknowledged him by simply murmuring, "Santa."

"Ho, ho, ho." This was fun. "Now, you come right here, little girl and sit on Santa's lap." Mac took a hold of Grace's arm and pulled her down on his lap. The children howled with delight. The only thing keeping Grace from giving "Santa" a slug was the kids' joy.

Mac knew that. "Santa's" laughter had become real now. "Ho, ho, ho. Tell me what you want for Christmas, Miss Grace."

She pondered for a second and then returned, "World peace." She pushed her way off his lap and marched off.

"Ho, ho, ho. Now Miss Grace left before I got to give her a gift." The children began calling her back.

"Thanks Santa, but I don't want a candy cane."

"Oh, I haven't got a candy cane for you." Mac reached into the pocket of his suit and pulled out a sprig of mistletoe. The cheering in the little diner reached epic proportions. Grace was beet red now and felt like melting into the floor.

Mac slowly walked to her and held the mistletoe over them. Looking at the adorable little faces around her, she knew she couldn't disappoint them. She reached up to give Mac a kiss on the cheek. He turned at the last second and their lips met. The kiss was gentle and soft, lasting only a second or two.

The massive cheering from the children all faded away as Grace felt Mac's soft lips on hers. Her head was light, her senses humming as she felt the nearness of the man. The spicy aftershave that he wore held her captive as she breathed it in deeply. She realized that she had been avoiding this closeness with every fiber of her being, even though it had been inevitable.

Nothing had prepared her for the explosion that the mere joining of their lips would bring to her. Before she pulled him into her and took the kiss deeper—and make no mistake, she wanted to take the kiss deeper— she stepped back. For a brief second their eyes met. They were no longer Santa and Miss Grace.

They were no longer Mac and Grace, with all the complications that came with that. They were simply a man and a woman, with attraction shooting sparks all around them.

Grace suddenly remembered where she was—in a roomful of curious children. Furious, she turned away from Mac and headed towards the door to, hopefully, usher the children and their teachers out of the diner.

Then she would roast "Santa" alive!

Mac stood frozen to the spot where he had stood as he kissed Grace. He had only been teasing her when the world had slipped off its axis. How could a simple meeting of the lips cause a brain to stop working? He stood there in total amazement. The essence of Grace continued to flow through him. The sweetness that was inherent in her had touched him in that brief kiss. It was like a drug. And he could become addicted.

It made no sense. It was just a little kiss. Nothing more.

He wanted more.

Slowly turning, somewhere in his head he heard the children saying goodbye to him. He smiled and waved as the teachers quickly ushered them out of the diner. He kept watching them, waving, until they were down the street. Then he felt it—the tension. He moved just his eyes to see Grace standing at the door, stewing. This wasn't going to be pretty.

He turned to her and smiled sheepishly. "It looks like they had a good time. I bet you're tired. You probably want to go home and rest. The Spinuccis and I can handle everything until Sally gets here."

Grace just stood watching him. Yes, this was very bad. Concern for her health hadn't moved her, so he'd change his tactic and try lightness. "Grace, Grace. Don't look so bothered. Haven't you ever wondered what it would be like to kiss Santa?" He chuckled trying to lighten the mood.

No change. "All right, I probably shouldn't have done that but the kids loved it, didn't they? It was all for the kids."

"Oh, don't give me that crap. I no more believe that your performance was for the kids than I believe that you really want Hal's Diner to increase business by thirty percent." She walked right up to him and faced him toe-to-toe, hands on her hips. "I don't know what you're up to but I don't want any part of it. None of it!"

Grace stormed into her office and slammed the door, angry with herself, not for the kiss but for liking the kiss so much. Her hands trembled as she looked around her office for work to do. Placing her arms around herself, she walked over to the small window and looked out. What had he done to her? And all with a simple kiss. It was crazy!

Mac stood looking at the closed office door. His first thoughts were confusion. She thought he was up to something? Well, he was . . . sort of. All he wanted was that perfect photograph.

Then the confusion changed to anger as he thought about the morning. He had dressed up as Santa for the children; it had nothing to do with his hopes of a picture. He had simply wanted to give them a good time at Hal's. He knew that Grace would be swamped and thought his appearance as St. Nick would help out, that's all. And she was faulting him for that? How ungrateful. The kiss may have been a little over the top but it was a quick touch, not a tonsil hockey, make-out session.

Incensed, he pulled his hat and beard off and stomped to the office. Flinging the door open he marched in and was amazed at what he saw. She looked so vulnerable, so lost looking out the window. Mac's heart took a strange turn. He had a strong urge to go to her and just hold her. When she heard him and turned, daggers flying from her eyes, Mac's warm feelings evaporated.

He straightened his shoulders and said, "Would you kindly tell me what is wrong with dressing up like Santa and surprising a bunch of kids?"

"Nothing—"

"What is so wrong with trying to help you out by having a little diversion from the cookies and milk?"

"I didn't say that—"

"What's so wrong with giving candy canes out at Christmas? Is there anything inherently wrong with that?" Mac's voice was rising with each sentence.

"No, it's just—"

"So, it's the kiss that bothered you." Mac stopped ranting and smiled widely. "Well, well, well, it all makes sense now."

Grace frowned and said, "What do you mean?"

"It's clear as a bell. You were blushing. When we kissed you felt something. I should have known that my charms would eventually overtake you," he said smugly.

With her anger back in full force, Grace walked from the window to stand in front of Mac. "Why, you arrogant, egotistical, jerk! I didn't even mean to kiss you. All I wanted to do was give you a little peck on the cheek, not mouth-to-mouth!"

"But you enjoyed it. It was very evident that you wanted more."

Grace felt the heat come back into her cheeks. "Shut up! Just get out! Now!" She hated the way her pulse was racing, the way her eyes were filling. Mostly, she hated that Mac was right.

Seeing the moisture gather in her eyes, Mac felt like a clod. His voice lowered some. "Grace, there's nothing wrong with enjoying a kiss. You're human after all. I enjoyed it, too."

Grace turned, her back to him. "I just bet you did."

"No, really." He touched her arm. "It stunned me, I couldn't think for a few seconds."

"You're just saying that."

Mac's voice lowered and softened as he continued. "No, I'm not. I guess I was curious. That's why I turned my head so you'd kiss me on the lips. It was . . . nice."

Grace brightened. Maybe she still had the upper hand here. Turning, she said, "Well, well, well. So you wanted to kiss me. Come to think of it, you didn't move for five minutes after that kiss. I had no idea that my kiss would be so potent on you. *You're* the one that felt something, McCrae, not me. It was *my* charm that melted you."

Mac was uncomfortable now. "Grace, I think you're blowing the kiss all out of proportion."

Smiling, Grace said, "Really, am I now?"

"Yes. It was just a simple little kiss to amuse the children."

"Right, there's absolutely nothing between us. Never has been and never will be, so we can just end it at that, right?"

"Right!"

Without noticing it, the two had been getting closer and closer into each other's face. They both stopped, suddenly realizing that they were a mere breath away from their lips touching again. As if without a choice, Mac looked down at Grace's full, pouty lips. They were luscious and just waiting for him.

Grace saw the hunger in Mac's eyes. Her heart leapt inside her breast at the impact of it. She felt that she would die if their lips did not meet again. Now.

Mac's eyes looked up into hers and saw the desire. It was more than an engraved invitation to him. He lowered his head that fraction of an inch and touched her lips with his. Surely he wouldn't feel the earth move again.

He was right. It was exploding all around him now!

This time, without children or beard to hamper them, the kiss did go deeper. Grace whimpered slightly as Mac drew her into his arms, as close as the padding of the costume would allow. The touch of his tongue to hers sent her shivering. Feeling that and loving it, Mac contracted his arms around her. Grace reached her hands up his back, anchoring herself to him.

Lights and colors filtered through Grace's brain. Stars shone brightly, as she enjoyed the feel of being held and kissed. She could imagine staying in his arms just like this, forever. Well, minus the costume.

Mac wondered how he could have ever lived without this feeling before. It was the most pleasant buzz he could ever remember. Although he didn't want to let her go, he gently eased back to look at her. Grace's eyes had a glaze of wonder over them. They were a beautiful brown.

Not sad.

He smiled at her, that smile that she loved. Grace could feel her knees shaking at the impact of it. She dropped her arms and stepped back. The awkwardness of the moment returned as she struggled with what to say. Mac just stood there looking at her. "Well," she finally said.

"Well," he replied.

Grace nervously fingered her star necklace. "I guess that was bound to happen."

"I guess so."

Mac wasn't making this any easier. Grace looked at him, wanting to know what he was thinking. "Now that it happened, I guess the curiosity is gone and we can get back to work."

With his eyebrows lifted Mac asked, "Do I still have a job?"

"Of course." Grace smiled slightly at him. "Mac, I can't blame you for that kiss. It's very obvious that we both wanted it. It was lovely. But now we need to forget that it ever happened and just go on with life."

Mac couldn't help feeling a little hurt. It was more than a "lovely" kiss. He knew that Grace had felt the connection between them. It was so like her to deny those feelings.

However, Mac was practical enough to know that Grace was right. A relationship between them would never work. She was trying to get to New York and soon he would be back in Miami Beach. She still thought he was a drifter, which was fine by him. The best thing for both of them was to go back to the way things had been.

"I guess you're right." He turned to go back to the kitchen.

As he opened the door to leave the room, Grace called him. "It was very nice of you to show up as Santa and give the kids candy canes. Thank you."

Knowing how hard it was for Grace to express gratitude over his Christmas cheer, he looked over his shoulder and nodded. "You're welcome."

Mac stopped before leaving the room. "And Grace? It was a lovely kiss."

The woman on the phone could not stop laughing.

"And then you came in as Santa Claus?" Paula's booming laugh was infectious. "I'd have given a year's pay to see that, Junior."

"I was pretty awesome, if I do say so myself." Christmas was getting closer. He really needed that photograph and thought that perhaps his partner would have some ideas. "So what do you think, Paula? Any brainstorms?"

"Well, you could always use one of the pics you've already gotten. I took a look at the proofs you sent. They're gold, Stu. You could make a career of photographing that little town."

"I tell you, Paula, this place is a photographer's paradise. Besides the decorations, there are the houses themselves and the town. The people, the parks, the trails, the lake, the wildlife. It's amazing!"

"Sounds like you like Charity. We're not going to lose you, are we?"

"Not a chance. But I sure would like to get this one photo before leaving. It could be the most incredible photograph that I've ever taken.

I've already arranged it in my mind." Mac sighed heavily. "If I could only get the owner of the diner to let me decorate. It would be so perfect."

"I thought you were working on her? That's why you're busing tables."

"Yeah, but so far my ideas have fallen flat."

"I can't believe that the great womanizer of our time, Stuart McCrae can't get a woman to do what he wants."

Mac suddenly didn't like the sound of that. "Well, believe it. This babe's different. She's an Ebenezer Scrooge with a healthy dose of the Grinch thrown in just for fun." Mac knew that was exaggerating a little, but he didn't want Paula to have a clue about his true feelings for Grace. He wasn't sure himself.

"Must be a peach to work with."

"No, it's just this Christmas thing she's so ornery about. She's really very good to her employees. She's kind to all her customers and adores the kids that come in after school everyday. She's really very warm and beautiful and . . ." Catching himself he said, "It's just me she has the problem with. Me and Christmas."

Paula wasn't fooled. The tone in Mac's voice convinced her that this woman was different. She loved her already for not falling down at Mac's feet. But the restrained passion that Paula could hear in Mac's voice for the woman concerned her.

"Hey, how about I come up? I could meet this woman; maybe convince her to put up decorations just for our shot. Woman to woman. What do you say?"

Mac thought about that. "It might not be a bad idea. When can you get away?"

"It won't be until next week. I've got appointments until next Wednesday."

"Not until then?" Mac complained.

"Sorry, McCrae. I'm working my butt off for you here. But if you'd like me to drop everything and come running to fix your problem I could—"

"No," Mac sighed. "I'll keep pitching. Just get here when you can."

"Will do." She absolutely would. She wanted to check out this woman who had captured her elusive partner's attention.

"Okay, kids. Is everyone clear on what to do?" Mac smiled at the group of young, eager, and slightly richer faces before him.

Mac had had an epiphany. The way to get to Grace was through the children. She loved them, catered to them, and would give them anything. He had tried before mentioning that the children would love Christmas candy and that hadn't work. So why not use actual children to do the convincing? The plan was brilliant!

It was the week before Christmas and school was out for the holidays. Mac had run across a group of excited youngsters in a park one morning as Noel and he had been taking shots of the sleepy little town. He had recognized the kids from afternoons at the diner.

They all had eagerly stopped playing to greet him. That's when he had his brilliant idea.

With a fresh new five-dollar bill in each of the ten children's pockets, they walked over to the diner. Among the kids was Holly, Noel's little sister. Glad to see her adored big brother, she walked with him, holding his hand. Noel looked down and grinned at the bright smile on his sister's face. Mac saw this. Noel's mood had been better since they had had their little chat. Whatever had been bothering him seemed to ease up. Mac was glad.

They made a quick stop at the hotel, so Noel could run Mac's equipment up to his room. While they waited, Mac felt a slight tug on his sleeve and saw Holly looking up at him.

"Mr. Mac?"

Looking down at the child Mac couldn't help smiling. She looked like a little pixie, so small and delicate, with her hair in two messy braids, her two front permanent teeth trying to come in, and a small dimple on the left side of her face. Mac couldn't resist. He reached down and scooped her up into his arms. "Yes, Miss Holly?"

She giggled and held on to him. "Do you think Miss Grace will like our idea?"

"Why of course! You know how much Miss Grace loves all of you. I'm sure she'll like the idea."

Holly thought about this. "I think she's starting to like Christmas. After all, my friend

Kimmie said that she saw Miss Grace kiss Santa Claus. Right on the mouth!"

Mac tried very hard not to laugh. He set Holly back down and then looked at the other children. "Now, you remember what you're going to say?" Little heads nodded. "And you remember the looks I showed you?" They all gave pouty, sad looks. "Excellent! I don't think I could resist giving all of you anything you asked for if you looked at me like that."

A little seven-year old boy with an especially pouty look said, "Then why don't you give us each another five-dollar bill?"

Mac laughed. "Wise guy! You know, Kyle, when you get older, I'll probably be working for you!" The child smiled at the compliment. "You're all clear on leaving my name out of this, right?" Heads nodded again. "I don't want anyone mentioning my name. It could . . . influence Miss Grace."

Noel came running back into the lobby and they were off. At the diner, Mac ordered hot chocolates for each of the kids and went back into the kitchen. He tried to stay close to the kitchen door to hear what went on in the dining room.

The breakfast crowd was gone and Grace was getting ready for lunch. Since school had let out, the natural schedule of the diner had changed. There was a mix of locals and tourists there throughout the day. Mealtimes were especially heavy. The afternoon visits by the children had ceased as they came intermittently during the day. Grace was glad to see the little group this morning.

"So, how's everything going, guys?" She asked as she poured the creamy, hot drink into mugs for them.

"Fine," they all muttered.

"Can I have lots of whipped cream on mine, Miss Grace?" Kyle asked.

"Sure, if I can hear the magic word."

Kyle rolled his eyes. Grown-ups! "Please," he said sweetly.

Grace smiled. She added an extra dollop of whipped cream to all the mugs and then enjoyed watching them sip their drinks. Turning to fill the napkin dispensers she asked, "What are you all up to today?"

The children looked at each other as if not sure how to begin. Noel decided to take the lead. "The park, right?" he said looking at the others. "Playing in the park."

"Oh, well, it's a good day for that. The weathermen said it will be sunny and in the low seventies for a few days."

It was quiet again. Then Kyle said, "Miss Grace, do you have any candy canes to sell?"

"No, Kyle. But I believe that you'll find them at the Main Street Market." She continued filling the canisters.

"How come?" Grace looked up to see Holly's eyes staring up at her.

"How come what, sweetheart?"

"How come you don't have candy canes to sell?"

Grace was stumped. She didn't have an answer. That is, she didn't have an answer other than that she hated Christmas. "I . . . didn't order any this year."

Another child said, "But you don't have *any* Christmas candy here."

Another said, "And you don't have any Christmas music."

"And no lights, or garland, or Christmas trees," said another.

Grace looked at the sea of sad faces in front of her. They were just kids with kid-sized problems. How could they ever understand how she felt, the grief that she experienced when she was reminded of this time of year?

But she loved them dearly and would never want to hurt them. At the same time she wanted to be honest with them. She set down the napkin dispenser and worried her hands together. "It's hard to explain, kids. It's just something that I don't do. It . . . hurts my heart a great deal to . . . celebrate Christmas."

"Should you go to the hospital or a doctor to get something for that?" Kyle asked.

Grace chuckled sadly and placed a hand on her chest. "No, it's not my beating heart. It's my feeling heart, darlin'. I just can't bring myself to celebrate."

"We'd be happy to put decorations up for you, Miss Grace," Noel volunteered. All the kids added their enthusiastic agreement.

"You wouldn't have to do a thing," Holly added.

Then the other children began added their own ideas. "We could hang wreaths on the doors." "And candles in the windows." "I could put bows up all over the outside." "I could string lights on the outside bushes." Something about that last remark grabbed Grace's attention.

Getting very excited, Kyle said with a raised voice, "And we need a giant Santa Claus to stand out in front, maybe twenty feet tall!" He reached his hand high above his head. All the other kids stopped talking and looked at Kyle. "Well, it'd look cool," he defended.

"I bet it would help business. More people would come in and order something if the place was decorated real nice," Noel added.

The edges of Grace's mouth lifted slightly. Everything was starting to make sense now. The lights on the bushes. The increase in business. And the children had all come in with Mac. Now, wasn't that such a coincidence.

Grace thought carefully about what her next words should be. She casually leaned over the counter to talk with the children. "So, you'd all like for Hal's Place to be decorated for Christmas." They all nodded and cheered. "You think everyone in town would like that?" They continued nodding. "And Mayor Scott and the local businesses would like that," she said as if she were thinking. The kids now automatically nodded as they drank their hot chocolate. "And the tourists. We can't forget about the tourists, can we?" The kids agreed.

Into the little plot by now, Grace rested her elbows on the counter and leaned over them. "What about Mr. Mac? You know, he loves Christmas a great deal. Do you think he'd like the place to be decorated?" The kids smiled broadly and nodded. Without missing a beat, she continued, "So how much did he pay you to come in today?" she casually asked.

"Five dollars," Kyle said without thinking.

"Oh, really?" Grace said as her face began to tighten.

Noel blanched as the other kids continued drinking. He thought he saw steam start to come out of Grace's ears. The jig was up. "Come on, kids. We need to get back to the park."

Grace looked at Noel. She knew. "That's all right, Noel. I'll keep you guys out of the line of fire." And with that, she tore off her apron and headed towards the kitchen. "McCrae!"

She was out for blood.

CHAPTER SIX

Muttering a bad word under his breath, Mac hurried away from the closed kitchen door where he had been listening. He grabbed a trashcan and headed out the side door that lead to the service area.

The swinging kitchen door flew open. "McCrae!" Grace stormed in with fire in her eyes. She looked around the kitchen, in the storage areas, in the pantry, even in the walk-in refrigerator and freezers. "Come on, you coward, I know you're here!"

Glancing down, she saw that a trashcan was missing. She stomped over to the door and looked out the window to see Mac taking his time emptying the trash. "All right, McCrae, it's time we had it out," she said under her breath. Opening the door she walked over to where Mac was, folded her arms, and stood there with a small, tight smile on her face.

Mac continued his work as if the future of civilization depended on it. After a while, he turned to look up at Grace. He knew that he wasn't going to get out of this one. "Hi," he casually said.

"Hi," Grace returned.

When she didn't say anything else, Mac said, "Did the kids like their hot chocolate? Just take the cost from me, okay?"

"Oh, Mr. McCrae. That's not all I'm going to take from you."

"Why, Miss Hudson. You're not going to get frisky with me here by the trashcans, are you?" he asked.

"Don't even think it! How can you use the kids like that?" Grace raised her hand to silence him, "And please, I beg you, please don't try to deny that you sent those kids to talk me into decorating the diner."

Mac wiped his hands on the fronts of his pants. He looked into her flashing eyes and, even though he was in terrible trouble, he couldn't help thinking how pretty she looked. He owed her the truth.

At least some of it.

"Yeah, Grace, you caught me. I had the kids come in with the express purpose of talking you into putting up decorations and enjoying the Christmas season."

"You bribed them!"

"I prefer to think of it as hiring them." When Grace gave him her best smirk, he relented. "Okay, I bribed them. I don't think I scarred them for life."

"Mac, enough already about Christmas. I don't think it's that big a deal, and frankly, I've about had enough of your plotting and scheming. I really don't want to deal with it. It's not that important!"

"But I think it is. It obviously hurts you-"

"And that's my business! I'm not celebrating Christmas, that's final!"

"Just tell me why!" Mac's voice was fierce. The sudden demand made Grace freeze. Then in a low voice, filled with tenderness and concern, Mac continued, "Tell me why, Grace, and I won't ask you again."

Tears had unexpectedly come into Grace's eyes. She hadn't cried over this in a long time. "It's nothing," she whispered.

Mac walked to Grace and took both her hands. "It's something." His eyes held hers, and it hurt him deeply to watch her fight the tears trying to escape. In a gentle, calming voice he said, "Let's sit down."

Grace was so embarrassed by the tears that she said nothing. She wiped her eyes with her sleeve as Mac dropped her hands and pulled two crates over, helping her to sit on one as he took the other.

Again, he took her hands and looked at her. "Tell me."

Grace sighed, emitting a hiccup of emotion that for anyone else would be part of a good cry. Mac couldn't help but to admire the strength of the woman next to him.

After taking a breath, Grace began. "Ten years ago, I lived with my parents in Jacksonville. It was just the three of us. My dad had a job as a restaurant manager at a golf course. My mother was a stay-at-home mom. I thought we had a pretty average, ordinary life.

"That year we got ready for Christmas like we did every year. My mother was very big on Christmas. The house was always decorated just like a Currier and Ives painting. We always made cookies and gingerbread houses, always took some to our neighbors and the nursing home down the street from us."

"Sounds like a good mom," Mac said gently rubbing Grace's hands.

"Yeah, you'd think. Only that year I woke up on Christmas Eve to find that my 'good mom' had flown the coop. She was gone, never to be heard from again," Grace said bitterly.

Mac frowned. "Did you call the police?"

"No need. She left my dad a note. He wouldn't let me read it but he told me that it said she had to leave and don't try to find her." Then she chuckled without humor. "Merry Christmas."

"Grace."

The tears started to fall without Grace even noticing. She was looking straight ahead as if reliving that horrible Christmas years ago. "That Christmas it was just Dad and me. We went out for lunch since he had no desire to cook. We opened the presents that we gave each other and threw away the ones from her. I cried every night for weeks. I didn't know it was possible to hurt like that."

Mac continued to massage her hands in his. His heart went out to the fifteen-year-old girl suddenly without her mother. He didn't know what to say. Finally, he put his arm around Grace and pulled her close. He kissed the top of her head.

Grace continued. "My dad decided that we would just keep hurting if we stayed there so we sold everything, packed up the car, and came down to Charity to live with Ellen. She took us in." Grace remembered with fondness the love that Ellen had showered on the confused teenaged girl.

"Dad bought the diner and changed the name to Hal's Place. He set to work to make it the best restaurant ever. He worked night and day to do that, although if the truth were told, he was really working to forget.

"He never forgot. I think in the end that's what killed him." Grace's voice cracked with the statement. "Now, every time I think about Christmas, I think about my mother and how she walked out on us." The emotions were now raw and visible on Grace's face and in her voice. "Sometimes I think I'd like the opportunity to spit in her eye for what she did to us and then sometimes I want to just ask her why, why, why Mom . . ." Then Grace broke down and started sobbing uncontrollably.

Moved beyond words, Mac pulled Grace into his lap and held her tightly. He rocked back and forth and kept kissing her head. How could he begin to know the pain that this woman had been through? And each time he had confronted her with Christmas, he had in some way brought back all the pain.

He felt like a horrible incarnation of the ghost of Christmas past.

They stayed like that a long time. Mac didn't know what Grace's past years had been like but he did know that this cry was good for her. He held her tightly through it.

Grace wrapped her arms around Mac, accepting the comfort. She nestled her head in his chest and breathed deeply. Maybe she would be ashamed of her outburst later but for right now, she wanted the strength that she felt from him.

When he thought she could handle it, Mac whispered, "I'm sorry, honey. So, so sorry."

Grace closed her eyes, enjoying the closeness. "Okay," she said against his chest.

Mac held Grace tightly to him, as if daring anyone to hurt her again. He tenderly stroked her hair. A warm sensation flooded his body as he felt the strong urge to protect this woman. He looked down at her and realized how important she had become to him. It wasn't supposed to happen like this. He was supposed to get his picture and then go home. But how could he leave this special woman? He would just have to do it. Leave and head back to Miami Beach before this went any further.

He was debating with himself when Grace looked up at him with big brown eyes filled with a gratitude that he had not seen before. And he was reminded how beautiful she was.

"Thank you, Mac. I think I really needed to vent," she said breathlessly as her eyes skimmed his face.

Mac could feel his heart stutter and then beat harder. What was she doing to him? He would leave, he would. But he had to have another kiss first. "You can vent to me anytime,

Grace." His head bent towards her just a fraction to see if she wanted the kiss that he had to have.

Her face lifted to his, eager to accept his lips. The contact was soft and gentle for about a second and then a passion and a fire took them both over. Mac reached his hand over the side of her face and threaded his fingers deep in her silky hair. His other arm wrapped tightly around Grace's waist, pulling her closer. Grace felt her body crush against Mac in a new and delicious way. Automatically, her arms tightened around him.

She felt free. She felt cleansed. She felt reborn. Maybe it was partly in the telling of her hurt, something she hadn't told anyone in years. But it was more than that. It was sharing something so personal and being totally accepted.

Grace knew that Mac was not the kind of person that would leave her on Christmas Eve. He cared about her. Who cares that his only job was a dishwasher for a small diner. His loving character was what was important.

Her mouth avidly sought his with a renewed energy. She covered his face, his ear, his jaw with little kisses, delighting when she drew a soft moan from him. If nothing else ever happened between them, she would live on this moment, this awareness of acceptance for the rest of her life.

Mac was dying. He was just plain dying. This woman that had tempted his senses since he had looked up into her big sad eyes, was now actively kissing him. In the past, he would have taken the affection without qualms and then moved on to the next town. Something was different here and he wasn't sure what it was.

He directed Grace's lips back to his for one last long, draining kiss. Then he slowly pulled back, looking at her face. Her eyes stayed closed and Mac smiled knowing that she was enjoying that last taste of his lips on hers.

When Grace opened her eyes, Mac's smile was the first thing she saw.

How perfect!

Softly Mac said, "Are you okay?"

Grace began to come back to reality. She sat up straight and wiped her eyes with her hands. "Yes." After taking a deep breath, she whispered, "Thanks."

"No problem," he said.

But there was a big problem and Mac had no idea on earth how he was going to solve it.

Something was different about Grace. Ellen just couldn't put her finger on it. Ellen watched Grace as she cashed out the register for the day shift. She had been like a mother to Grace for the past ten years and she watched over the younger woman like a hawk. The slightest of smiles on Grace's face told her that something had happened. There was a lightness to Grace's countenance, a spring to her step, and an eagerness in her work that Ellen couldn't remember seeing before.

Thinking that she should find out, she wandered over to the checkout counter, washcloth in hand, and began cleaning the surface near the register.

"How'd we do today?" she casually asked.

"Not bad. I think with the extra people in town we'll have a pretty good month. How have the nights been?"

"Steady. Good." Ellen continued her pretense of cleaning. "You certainly seem in a chipper mood today."

"Yes, I feel pretty good. Hey, did we get that shipment of paper products?"

"Huh?" Ellen was looking at Grace, trying to get a bead on what was different about her. "Ah, no. They haven't come yet."

"Oh shoot. I'll go make a call and see if they can't get them out today." Grace finished her work at the register and looked up to see Ellen studying her. "What is it?" she asked.

Ellen shook her head. "Something's different. What's happened?"

Grace laughed. "You are quick to the point. I don't know what you mean."

"No, I think you do." Ellen dropped her cloth and folded her arms. "Now spill it."

Looking confused, Grace said, "Nothing's happened."

"You look refreshed. Your eyes are wide and bright. I even heard you humming a tune. It's not like you to be so happy and . . . glowing."

"Thank you?" Grace frowned. "Am I usually miserable and pale?"

"Usually."

"Gee, thanks. I guess I'm glad we're family. No telling what you'd say about me if we weren't." Grace took her paperwork and moved towards the office.

Ellen followed her. "Now Grace, darlin', I love you like you were my own daughter, you know that. And because we're so close I can see that something's happened. Now, are you going to tell me or am I going to have to hound you night and day until you do?"

Grace hesitated as she looked at Ellen. Then she walked into the office saying, "It's really not that big a deal. It's just—"

The door to the office closed and Ellen was seated on the folding chair, elbows on the desk with her face in her hands ready to listen.

"Why don't you have a seat, Ellen?" Grace said sarcastically.

"Come on, come on. I haven't got all day."

Grace set her papers on her desk and sat. "Yesterday I . . . well I . . ."

"Yes?"

She sighed. "I told Mac all about my mother. I hadn't meant to but he made me so mad, trying to get me to celebrate Christmas. We were both yelling at each other trying to make our points and he pushed me to tell him what happened."

Her expression now one of sympathy, Ellen reached for Grace's hand. "Aw, baby," she whispered.

"No, it was a good thing. I broke down, Ellen. I haven't cried over my mother in years. I guess the bitterness and anger just grew inside and stayed bottled up. It was such a release to let it out. I feel, in a way, cleansed." Then in a little voice Grace said, "He held me and just let me cry. He didn't try to say anything witty or reasonable. He just let me be."

Ellen smiled. "He's a wise man."

Then Grace looked up at her aunt. "Then he kissed me."

"Aw, baby," Ellen dropped her hand and stood to pace.

"I know what you're thinking, Ellen. I think so, too. It can't go anywhere. There's no future for Mac and me. We're heading in different directions."

"Good. Then you don't have to hear a lecture from me," Ellen said. Grace looked down at her hands. "No, Grace. I would like nothing better than for you to find a nice man and settle down, but Mac isn't that man."

With her head tilted Grace said, "I thought you weren't going to lecture me."

"What can I say, it slipped out of me. Just tell me one thing." Ellen took a breath. "How do you feel about Mac?"

Grace saw the concern in Ellen's eyes and said a quick prayer of thanks. Her life had been hard in the past ten years but she could not have imagined surviving without her beloved aunt.

As Ellen waited for an answer, Grace tried to think of a satisfactory answer to give her. She couldn't lie. Not to Ellen. For one thing it wouldn't be right. For another thing, Ellen would know. She always did know when Grace was lying. How could she tell Ellen that she didn't have any feelings for Mac when she knew that was a bold-faced lie? She opened her mouth to answer. "Ellen . . . I— "

The loud bang in the kitchen grabbed both women's attention. "What in the world?" Ellen was running out the office door with Grace on her heels instantly. When they got to the kitchen, they saw the Spinucci's facing each other, a spilled pan on the floor, dark smudges on each other's face and aprons. Bruiser stood at the nearby island, chopping vegetables and not paying attention to anything going on.

"All right, folks. Just what is going on in here?" Grace asked with authority.

"Ah, Miss Grace. Miss Ellen. This woman. She's ah gonna be the death of me yet. She tries to ruin my mama . . . may she rest in peace," Sal crossed himself, "my mama's gingerbread."

"Sal! Mama Spinucci live in New York City!"

"That's ah what I mean. She live in New York City. May God protect her."

"You are a foolish man, Sal Spinucci. No one puts parsley in gingerbread?" Loretta yelled while reaching for a towel.

Grace looked at Ellen and with a wince mouthed the word parsley.

"And you have been eating it for all these years and loving it. Now ah you tell me no parsley. I must have my parsley!" Sal stomped to the other side of the kitchen and grabbed a towel for himself.

As they were on opposite sides of the room, Grace saw this as her opportunity to intervene. "Okay, let's everyone cool off for a moment." As the couple faced each other with venom in their eyes, Grace threw up her hands like a policeman stopping traffic. "Really, guys. Let's talk this thing out."

At that moment, Noel came in carrying a large box of toys. He put the box on the floor by his feet and surveying the damage said, "Whoa, what happened in here?"

"She attack me, she did. All because I make ah better gingerbread than her," Sal answered.

"What sane person puts parsley in ah their gingerbread?" Loretta asked.

"My mama, that's ah who!"

"I repeat. What *sane* person puts parsley in ah their gingerbread!"

As the two began to yell again, Grace sighed and put her fingers in her mouth and blew. The loud whistle got the attention of the fighting pair. "How about we have an impartial judge taste the batter? Noel? Come over here and taste this."

"Oh, Miss Grace, I'm not really the best taster." Although he was only fifteen, Noel was smart enough to know that he didn't want to get between the Spinucci's and their cooking. "I'm looking for Mac. I've got this box of toys for him."

Intrigued, Grace asked, "What does Mac need with toys?"

"They're not for him. The Presbyterian Church is collecting toys for the homeless shelter. He, my dad, and I are taking them over this afternoon."

Grace was touched. Every time she thought she had discovered all of Mac's good points another seemed to crop up. Smiling at Noel she said, "Mac took off a couple of hours ago. I'm sure he'll be back soon."

"So, is he gonna taste my delicious recipe or not?" Sal said getting the attention back on the problem at hand.

"Why don't you taste it, Miss Grace?" Noel was a much smarter boy than Grace gave him credit for. She gave him a knowing smirk.

The roar of a motorcycle coming down the street drew everyone's attention to the dining room and out the front windows. "There's Mac now," Grace said trying to think of a way to get out of the kitchen. Then an idea hit her. "Hey, why don't we have him taste it?"

The Spinuccis agreed as the unsuspecting Mac entered the side door of the kitchen carrying a bag of toys. "Hey," he said to no one in particular. "Oh, hey Noel. I see you brought some toys."

"Yeah. My dad will be along in a minute. Maybe we'd better go wait for him out front," Noel said with beseeching eyes.

Unaware of the impending danger Mac said, "Let me just get this dishwasher started

before I leave. Whoa, what's all this mess?"
Then looking around, he got an idea of what he
had walked into.

Enjoying his discomfort, Grace walked
over to him and patted his shoulder. "It seems
that the Spinucci's can't agree on a gingerbread
recipe. They need a taster and we've
volunteered you to help them out."

Sensing a no-win situation, Mac tried to
worm out of the job. "Gee, I'd like to Sal and
Loretta, but . . ." He saw Noel with the box of toys
and walking over he put his sack of toys on top of
the box and picked both up. "Noel and I have a
delivery to make. In fact, I think I see our ride
now." Mac scanned outside, hoping Noel's father
was coming down the street.

"You know, I think what you're doing is
such a worthy cause, I'll join you," Grace said,
quickly moving out of the kitchen to grab her
sweater and purse.

As the three hurried out front, Sal said,
"But who's ah gonna test the recipe?"

"Hi, honey!" Mayor Scott said, coming
through the front door and seeing Ellen through
the kitchen pass through. She seemed to melt as
Howard walked into the kitchen and put his arm
around her, giving her a kiss on the cheek.

"Hi," she said breathlessly forgetting the
Spinuccis, and gingerbread, and the whole world
in general.

"I know. We'll get the mayor to sample
the batter," Loretta said excitedly.

"Excellent idea, Loretta. Then we can let everyone know that Charity's most important citizen loves ah my mama's recipe!"

Howard looked up and examined the scene. *This is not good*, he thought. He grabbed Ellen's hand thinking of how they could possibly escape when Sal dipped a spoonful of batter from the cake tin and, smiling, walked over to the mayor.

"Why don't we get Big Jed and Little Jed to do this? I think I saw them outside?" Howard said as the large spoon of dark batter loomed before him.

He squeezed Ellen's hand as if to say farewell to her.

CHAPTER SEVEN

The Presbyterian Church was filled with people. Friends and neighbors had joined together to make up Christmas baskets for less fortunate families in the area. Noel's father had dropped his passengers off with their toy donations to contribute to the community effort. Entering the sanctuary, Grace was pleased to be greeted with warmth and affection. There were tables set up where busy workers were putting together the beautiful baskets.

The three were directed to an empty table and given instructions. They spent the rest of the afternoon putting the baskets together and chatting. Grace was having such a good time. It felt so good to so something for others. Mac could see the peace in her face. He smiled at her as she tied a big bow on a basket. She was enjoying herself. He had noticed how the people at the church liked and respected her. He wasn't surprised.

The sun was setting when they finished up and left the church. Noel insisted that he could walk home alone and set out. Mac looked at Grace, and feeling like a shy schoolboy said, "Let me walk you home."

Feeling like a shy schoolgirl, Grace said, "Okay."

They walked in silence, enjoying the coolness of the air and the quietness of the early evening. After a while Grace said, "I really enjoyed helping out at the church."

Mac smiled. "I know they appreciated your help."

"Thanks for letting me tag along," Grace said quietly, looking down.

He couldn't help himself. She was so cute. Mac walked closer to Grace and took her hand. "You're welcome." They walked on in contented silence.

"How did you know about the event at the church?" Grace asked.

"Whenever I'm in an area, I always look around for places I can plug in to. You know, do little things to help out. I figure a place gives me so much that I want to give back."

"How do you mean they give you so much?"

Be careful here, McCrae. Mac couldn't tell her how thankful he always was for the great photo opportunities that towns gave him. He had to think of something else. "Well, for the most part people have been really nice to me. I just like to be nice back."

Grace smiled. "That's a good thing. It's a very good way of looking at life. How did you learn that?"

"My grandma taught it to me." Mac's heart warmed just in thinking of his beloved grandmother.

Intrigued, Grace said, "Tell me about her."

Mac's smile was wide now and beaming. "She was the greatest lady that ever lived. You would have loved her. She was a little thing, maybe five feet tall, with beautiful silver hair for as long as I remember. Her voice carried authority." Mac chuckled. "I remember watching with awe at the way she could get big, husky workmen to do her bidding around the house." He stopped short of talking about the maids and butlers. "She pretty much raised me."

Trying not to be too inquisitive, Grace asked, "No mom or dad?"

"Yeah, I have a mom and dad but they . . . were busy working all the time." Jetting all over the world was more like it. "They're good people but they just didn't have enough time for a child."

Grace felt sad for him. "But you had your grandmother."

The smile returned. "Yes, I did." Mac sighed. Deciding to take a chance here he added, "She always celebrated Christmas in a big way. We had it all; lights, tree, presents, decorations." He stopped to see if Grace was listening. She was. "We made every Christmas cookie known to man and ate almost as many as we gave out. The house smelled so good that time of the year between the real Christmas tree, hard to get in Miami by the way, the cookies, the gingerbread. It was heaven."

That probably explains his obsession with Christmas decorations. "That must have been fun for you. It must be nice to have such good memories."

"It is. And it's all because of Grandma. She had a kindness that was so deep, so giving that everyone loved her."

"Did she die, Mac?" Grace asked in a low voice.

Quietly Mac said, "Last spring. She had been sick. We all knew she was dying." He looked straight ahead into the distance. "She died in her sleep, peacefully. Just as she lived."

Grace squeezed his hand wanting so much to bring comfort to this special man. "I'm sorry. It must have been hard."

Mac turned back to Grace. His eyes were sad as he smiled at her. "You're never prepared for a loved one to die. But she lived a good life. She was able to see me raised." He nodded his head. "She was ready to go." Then looking up into the darkening sky, he said, "Grandma told me that when she went, she was going to ask God to let her be a star so she could look down and keep an eye on me."

Grace stopped in her tracks forcing Mac to do the same. Amazement filled her face as she fingered the star necklace that she always wore, looking down at it. "That's the same thing that my father told me. When he knew that he was going to die, he had Ellen get me this necklace to wear so that I would know that he was always with me."

Mac took her necklace in his hand and looked at it. Then gazing at her large, soft eyes he forgot Christmas decorations and pictures and thought only of Grace. "It looks like we've got two stars watching over us."

Their eyes met and held.

Knowing he should lighten the moment, Mac said, "Hey, how about a ride?"

"Huh?"

Pulling her by the hand, Mac started walking again, this time briskly. "You don't have to work tonight. How about letting me take you for a ride on my Harley?"

"I don't know, Mac. I've got some paperwork to do and—"

"Do you really want to go back to Hal's just yet? The Spinuccis may still be waiting for a tasting volunteer." Both Mac and Grace shuddered. "Besides. You're not afraid, are you?" he said with a smirk.

Grace rolled her eyes at him. "Really, Mac. Resorting to juvenile dares?"

He laughed. "Of course. So, did it work?" he asked with a twinkle in his eye.

With a laughing smile, Grace said, "Do you have an extra helmet?"

The next day, Grace was busy decorating a chocolate cake when little Holly came in and hopped up onto a stool. "Afternoon, Miss Grace."

"Afternoon, Holly." Grace smiled at the little girl and wiped her hands with the rag she had tucked in her apron. "What can I get for you today?" Grace was happy. She couldn't remember the last time she had been this happy. Was it when she graduated from college or high school? No, she couldn't remember feeling this way before.

The motorcycle ride with Mac the night before had been exhilarating. She had laughed as the wind rushed over them and the night shined above them. Holding on tight to Mac, she had rested her head against his back, enjoying the smell of his leather jacket, the essence that was Mac. The roar of the engine below her had given her a feeling of protection, as it seemed to emit power and strength. It had felt so good for power to come from some source other than herself. The ride had truly relaxed her.

Then Mac had walked her to her apartment on Main Street. At her door, he had kissed her gently, sweetly, with no expectations. Then smiling, he left her. She could still feel the thrill of the soft kiss, could still feel Mac's soft lips meeting hers with tender affection. Half the night had been spent thinking of Mac and dreaming about "what ifs." When they both reached the diner that morning they had said good morning to each other sharing a secret smile. Now, Mac worked quietly in the kitchen while she thought of him.

"Miss Grace?"

Grace startled, coming back from her thoughts to Holly. "I'm sorry, Holly. I didn't hear what you said."

"My daddy gave me money for a scoop of ice cream in a bowl. Could I have it with nuts and whipped cream please?"

"Of course, you can, honey. Rocky road, right?" When Holly nodded, Grace added, "And because you are such a special customer, I'll even add one of Miss Ellen's giant chocolate chip cookies to it."

Holly's eyes grew wide with wonder. "Oh boy!"

Grace chuckled as she set to work on Holly's order. "Are you glad to be out of school, Holly?"

"I guess. I miss my teacher, though. And Maddie and Rachael and Ali and Peyton."

"Wow! You've got a lot of friends, there."

"And Marie and Lauren and Katelyn." Grace put the dish of ice cream with the cookie in front of Holly. "Oh, boy!" she said again and began to dig in.

Grace loved all the children in Charity but Holly held a special place in her heart. There was something about her that connected to Grace's heart. Finding that she wanted to linger with Holly, Grace pulled her cake down by Holly to work on it there.

"I've been seeing a lot of Noel lately. It seems he's developed quite a friendship with Mac."

Smacking her lips at the cool texture of the rocky road ice cream, her favorite, Holly said, "Yeah. Mr. Mac is a nice man. He came to see us at our house. He asked Daddy if Noel could help him."

"Help him with what, Holly?"

Holly stopped for a second. She knew she wasn't supposed to tell something but she wasn't sure what it was. But surely Miss Grace was okay. Holly wouldn't get in trouble telling her what she knew. "Noel is helping Mr. Mac with a project. They go around the town and take pictures."

"Really?" Grace set down her knife and looked at the ceiling thinking. Then turning back to Holly she asked, "Why are they taking pictures of Charity?"

"I don't know. I guess Mr. Mac just likes to take pictures." Holly took a big bite of the cookie and with crumbs falling from her mouth she added, "He's really good at it."

"Yes, I know."

The question in Grace's eyes had Holly frowning. Had she said too much? She didn't want her good friend Mr. Mac to get into trouble so she said, "Mr. Mac has been so nice to Noel. We've been worried about him."

Concern filled Grace's eyes then and she asked, "Why, Holly?"

"Noel wasn't too happy. Even with Christmas coming he seemed so sad. Then he started helping Mr. Mac and he's happy. He and Mr. Mac are going all around town taking pictures and if they see someone they can help, they help. Noel even helped me put my Barbie doll's head back on yesterday."

"What a nice brother." For a moment Grace thought about how her father had helped her put Barbie doll heads back on when she was little. A little lump formed in her throat thinking of the man. "Well, I'm glad, Holly. You're very lucky to have a brother like Noel."

She took another bite of ice cream, finishing the bowl. "That's what my daddy says." Holly hopped down from the stool and walked to the checkout counter. Reaching into her pocket she pulled out a five-dollar bill and gave it to Grace who had followed her. "Could I have five cents worth of penny candy, too? It's for my mama."

"She's a lucky woman to have such a considerate daughter," Grace said as she rang up the purchase.

"Yes ma'am." Then taking her bag of candy, she said, "I love my mama, very much."

The sharp pain that Grace anticipated coming as Holly talked about her mother was not as bad as was expected. Looking at Holly's sweet little face, Grace was filled instead with longing—longing to say those words to her mother and mean them, to feel the emotion that Holly had. Smiling sadly, Grace said, "Good for you, honey."

Happy with her purchase, Holly bounced out of the door. "Bye, Miss Grace."

"She's a cute, little girl, isn't she?" Ellen came up behind Grace and put her hands on her shoulders. Having just gotten to the diner, Ellen had heard the exchange and felt the pain radiating from Grace.

Grace acknowledged the comfort Ellen was giving her. She turned and hugged the older woman with all her strength. "I love you Ellen, very much."

Ellen knew that Grace was telling her that she considered Ellen as her mother. Ellen returned the hug and kissed Grace's cheek. "I love you too, sweetheart."

Then wanting to ease the emotion swarming them, Ellen asked, "So did you hear how the gingerbread tasting went yesterday?"

Grace smiled. "I heard Howard got the Jeds to do the tasting and the vote was one for Loretta and one for Sal. Is that right?"

"Yeah. Who'd have thought that the Jeds were smart enough to know that they'd need to split the vote?" Both women giggled. "How'd we do today?"

"Not bad. Here are the receipts. I was just going to enter them and take a deposit to the bank."

"Great. Hey listen. The Baptist Church is doing the Singing Christmas Tree and Howard's got tickets for tomorrow night. Could we switch shifts tomorrow so I can go with him?"

With a smug smile, Grace said, "Sure." And then to please herself, she said, "You seeing a lot of the mayor?"

Ellen smiled smugly. "Every chance I get."

Grace whooped. "Tell me more. Oh, am I old enough to hear this, auntie?" She laughed.

Ellen had always hated when Grace called her "auntie" and Grace knew it. "You watch your tongue, missy, or I'll leave you in the dark." Ellen knew that Grace hated to be called "missy."

"Sorry." No longer interested in business, Grace pulled up a chair, sat, and said, "Proceed."

Looking down at her hands, Ellen smiled and slightly blushed. "He's a good man, Grace. I enjoy myself so much when I'm with him. And when I'm not, I find myself thinking about him."

Grace could relate. She was having trouble not thinking about Mac.

"He's so kind and sweet. We have lunch almost everyday. Sometimes he'll come by the diner at night and we'll have a slice of cake and coffee together. We talk everyday." Ellen looked so dreamy.

"Sounds wonderful," Grace said.

Looking at her niece, Ellen said, "I know. So why do I have this fear that something bad's going to happen?"

Grace was immediately off her chair and embracing her aunt. "Aw, Ellen. Why do you think that?"

"Because I'm not a spring chicken. Second chances for love just don't come around for women my age."

"Nonsense. You're a beautiful, attractive woman. Any single man of intelligence would be able to see that, even if you can't."

"I guess I'm being silly."

"Yes, you are. Now stop thinking of all the things that could go wrong and just enjoy it, do you hear?"

"Yes ma'am," Ellen said sarcastically. Then a thought occurred to her. "You know, the singing Christmas tree will be performing for several nights. Would you like me to get you a couple of tickets?"

The tightness in Grace's chest that always came at the mention of Christmas wasn't as sharp. Maybe she was finally beginning to heal. Kissing Ellen's cheek and grabbing the deposit bag and receipts she said, "No, but thank you."

As Grace walked away, Ellen watched her. *Not there yet, but she's coming.* Then smiling, Ellen got to work.

"If you won't be needing me, Grace, I'll head on home now." Tom, the night cook, was putting on his jacket as Grace was cleaning the dining room.

"Yeah, go on, Tom," she called back to him as she scrubbed the tabletop of a booth. The night had been a busy one. It seemed that everyone that had been to see the singing Christmas tree had decided to stop in at Hal's for a piece of cake or pie and coffee afterwards. Everyone, that is, but Ellen and Howard. Grace smiled as she worked. She really liked where that was heading.

As she continued her work, she could hear Mac in the kitchen mopping the floor. It was so good to have him there. Not only had he helped the diner out in a big way but also his very presence seemed to make people happy. Especially Grace. She knew the day would come when he'd leave and it would be hard, but she'd survive.

Everyone left sometime.

Maybe she would be leaving soon, heading to the Big Apple to officially start her life. She felt like she'd been in limbo for so long, hiding her wants and desires underneath what she felt she had to do. It won't be long, she kept telling herself.

From the kitchen, she heard Mac begin to whistle "Rudolph the Red-Nosed Reindeer." Grace couldn't help smiling. Taking her washrag and pail of soapy water back to the kitchen, she said, "I can hear you, you know."

Mac's smile was wide and devastating. "I know."

Grace chuckled. As she emptied the bucket and wiped it out she said, "The front's all done, if you want to mop. I'll just be straightening things up in the pantry. Then she disappeared into the large room.

With Grace out of the kitchen and dining room, Mac turned on the radio in the kitchen to the "all Christmas, all the time" station to listen to Christmas carols while he finished his work.

He took the mop with two buckets, one with fresh soapy water and the other empty to collect dirty water, into the dining room and began working as the next Christmas carol came on the radio. He couldn't help it. He started singing.

Now, no one would suggest his voice could compete with Frank Sinatra, but he could carry a tune. That was what Grace noticed when she came out of the pantry. She closed the door and paused as she listened to the song.

Not that song.

Grace let her back rest against the door of the pantry as memories flooded her mind. Her throat got suddenly heavy. Her stomach ached as she listened to the beautiful song.

"Away in a Manger." The song that Grace's mother had sung to her every Christmas that she could remember. Every Christmas that she was there, anyway. Tears filled her eyes as she remembered the tender way that her mother had held her and sang softly in her ear. Grace could still smell her sweet perfume, could still feel her gentle arms around her. As she sniffed back the tears, Grace suddenly noticed that the overwhelming crushing sensation in her chest that usually accompanied all memories of Christmas was . . . not there. Yes, there was pain. Yes, there was sadness. But she wasn't falling physically ill over the experience. Interesting.

The song ended and Grace stayed where she was, thinking through all the emotions swirling through her body. Thankfully, the next song was "Frosty, the Snowman." Grace wiped the remaining tears from her eyes and took a deep breath in order to get control of herself.

Mac continued singing, this time trying to sing the old tune just like Jimmy Durante had sung the song in the old classic television show. Grace found herself smiling. She couldn't help it. Mac was doing such a bad impression of the famous version. A giggle slipped out followed by another. Grace was amazed at how Mac was able to get her to smile, to laugh.

To feel happy again.

Coming into the kitchen with the mop and two pails, Mac caught Grace leaning against the pantry doors laughing at him. "Everybody's a critic," he muttered.

Grace laughed harder. He watched her while he rinsed out the mop and the buckets. He loved her laugh. It was light, carefree. So unlike the person. Mac figured that Grace was letting go of her burdens when she laughed. He yearned to make her laugh again and again.

The next song on was a sultry saxophone version of "Have Yourself a Merry Little Christmas." As he put up the mop and buckets he walked over to Grace. "You're laughing at me, huh?"

With her hands over her mouth trying to conceal her giggles, Grace shook her head. Her eyes shone with amusement. They were beautiful.

"Well, just for that, you've got to dance with me." Mac took her hand and led her to the middle of the kitchen.

CHAPTER EIGHT

"What? Are you kidding? I'm not going to dance with you here in the kitchen!" Grace exclaimed.

"Sure you are," Mac said confidently as he enfolded her into his embrace and began swaying with her in time to the music.

The guy knew how to dance. Grace was constantly amazed at this man. His moves were smooth and rhythmic, causing Grace to go into a trance as she rested her head against his. It was a trance that she didn't want to come out of. She could smell the sweat of hard work on him along with a lingering hint of aftershave. Grace did love his aftershave. She was tempted to ask him what it was so she could keep some in her apartment to smell. And be reminded of him. How silly, she thought.

The dreaminess of the song continued as Mac drew her closer. "See, Christmas songs can be very enjoyable, can't they?" he quipped.

Deciding to enjoy herself, she looked up at him. "Well, I'm enjoying this one." Her eyes shined at him.

She was doing it to him again. Mesmerizing him with those expressive eyes. He could feel her heart beating against his. The desire in his soul for this woman continued to grow although he tried to tell himself that it was wrong. She was like an anchor, holding him steady. She was like an oak tree, drawing roots out of him that he didn't want. She was like a magnet, pulling him into her, body and soul.

She was like an answer to a question he had been asking for years but had been in no hurry to answer.

Until now.

They continued to dance, neither speaking, both looking into each other's eyes. When Grace lifted both arms to go around his neck, Mac moaned inwardly. Her nearness was addictive. He found himself wanting more of her. He decided. Tonight he would have more.

Grace watched the expression on Mac's face change from delight to hunger. It thrilled her at the same time that it frightened her. As he stopped dancing and lowered his lips to meet hers, she felt an incredible need. She shuddered, causing a groan to come from him. His lips were not gentle this time, but powerful. Intense. Ravenous.

Reveling in that need, Grace opened her mouth to him, letting him take the kiss deeper and deeper. His hands explored Grace's back with eagerness. Grace realized that she wanted his hands all over her. Her sigh of appreciation told Mac all he needed to know. With restraining passion and utmost care, he molded her against the long, hard line of his body. His hand slipped under her shirt and moved slowly up her side until he caressed just below her breast.

The breath in Grace's lungs seemed to clog in her throat as her excitement increased. She kissed him with renewed vigor wanting to feel everything with Mac. Her hands went to run through his gloriously unkempt, black hair. Mac's one hand rested on the small of her back, pushing her lean body into his while his other hand began kneading her breast.

The little moans that Grace made were driving him crazy. He wanted her so badly that the rational part of his brain that said this wasn't a good idea was irreparably and completely shut off.

The radio played another song, an upbeat version of "The Twelve Days of Christmas" but neither of them heard it. . Slowly, Mac undid the apron that Grace wore and let it slip to the floor. His hands came to the buttons on her blouse as she spread little kisses on his face. Grace's hands were on his hips now, massaging, enjoying the feel of his hard muscles. Mac looked into her eyes, wanting to see the needs and desires that he felt reflected in her eyes. He wasn't disappointed. With a huge sigh of contentment, Mac began kissing Grace's neck while he unbuttoned her blouse. His fingers itched to touch her, to feel the creamy white skin under his palms. To follow his hands with his mouth. He could already taste the sweetness.

Grace tried not to hold her breath. Never had a man aroused the emotions in her that Mac did. Her hands came around his hips and caressed his back, all the while moaning in enjoyment.

As Mac undid the last button and was starting to push the blouse away, his cell phone began to ring. He knew that ringtone. He had to take the call.

From far away in her conscious Grace thought she heard ringing. Then she realized it was a phone. She watched as Mac cursed and stepped away from her. He pulled a phone from his pocket. How did he have a cell phone? And not only a cell phone but also the latest model from a high-end cell phone company. This didn't make any sense. Grace pulled her blouse across her chest, suddenly cold.

"Hello," Mac snapped into the phone. He waited and listened. After a few "uh-huhs" and "yeahs" he said, "I'll be right there." He closed the phone and looked into the questioning eyes of Grace. "I've got to go. I'll walk you home."

He walked to the storage area and grabbed his coat. When he returned to the kitchen, he saw Grace in the same spot as when he left her. Her eyes were now a mixture of bewilderment and doubt. Mac damned himself for causing that.

After slipping on his jacket, he walked over to her and tenderly buttoned up her blouse. "Come on," he said softly. "Let's get your things and lock up."

Mac left Grace at the door of her apartment with a small peck on the cheek. As she saw him walk down the stairs and across the street to the hotel, she wondered what it was that he had to see to. Apparently he couldn't tell Grace. Why did that hurt her so much? They had no binds, only the attraction that they felt for each other. That wasn't quite true. He may have felt only attraction. Grace knew, she feared, that the attraction that she felt for him had already plunged into the realm of love.

Grace watched Mac go into the hotel. She had to get her bearings back. Had to get her priorities in order. Sell the restaurant. Move to New York. That's what she would concentrate on.

But even the excitement of the Big Apple wouldn't be able to help her forget the joy that she had found in Mac's arms.

Mac hurried into the lobby of the hotel. He looked around until he found an attractive brunette sitting in a high-backed cushioned chair looking exhausted. A smile instantly came to Mac's face. "Paula!"

At the sound of her name, the woman turned to see Mac. She stood and waited for him to reach her. Then with the love that they had developed over the years they embraced.

"How you doing, darlin'?"

"Much better, now that you're here," he said and kissed her warmly. Mac looked down into the face of his partner. Her brown eyes were shining as she grinned up at him. Mac noticed the thinness of her cheeks and wondered if she had been working so hard she was neglecting herself. Again. "Have you been eating, honey? You know you have to take care of your health."

"I know, Stu." Paula thought about how close she had come to death a few years ago. If Mac hadn't been in her life, she didn't know what she would have done.

"Your lungs giving you any problem?"

"No, I'm fine really. Just a little tired from the drive."

Mac decided to let the questioning go for now. "Have you got a room yet? I'd've been here to meet you if you'd told me when you were coming."

"Yes, I've got a room. Next door to yours. I told you I'd get here sometime this week, I just didn't know what day. Besides I was busy wrapping up the Florida Keys deal. I thought you'd want me to finish that up."

"Paula, I don't want to travel anymore, I told you that."

Paula smiled and taking his arm, began to move to the elevator. "I know, but the Keys are practically next door." Paula's eyes shone with the pleasure of making the deal. "We couldn't pass this up, Junior. The gift shop business alone will make you a millionaire."

"I'm already a millionaire."

"Well, I'm not. Indulge me." She punched the up button. Then standing there, her arm linked with his, she seriously looked at his face. "How are you really, Stu?"

"I'm fine."

"Still working on that diner lady to get the perfect shot?"

"Still plugging away." He thought about Grace. "I think she's weakening," he added, the corners of lips lifting slightly.

"Uh oh," Paula said as they walked into the open elevator. "That's what I was interrupting when I called you. I thought you sounded perturbed."

Laughing, Mac said, "Who says 'perturbed?' God, Paula, I've missed you." Then he gave her another kiss, one on the cheek this time.

"Right back at ya, kid. Now, tell me about this girl. Maybe I can help things."

The bell dinged as the elevator opened onto their floor. They walked to Paula's room as Mac sighed. "I think it would take me all night to explain Grace."

Paula opened her door and walked in, dropping the key on the television top. "Well, try."

As they sat, Mac began. "She's a hard worker. I've never seen anyone work as hard as Grace. She's at the diner at sunup and many days until they lock up, close to midnight. She's kind. She gives respect to everyone she deals with, from customers to employees to vendors. She's sweet. You should see her with the kids that come into the diner. She loves them and they love her right back."

"The girl sounds wonderful. I don't understand why she hates Christmas so much."

Mac sighed. "I don't think she'd want me to share the details but let's just say that she had a horrible Christmas about ten years back and has never forgotten it. Every time she sees a decoration she suffers."

Paula nodded in agreement. "Christmas can sometimes bring the sharpest pain known to man."

Turning to look at her, Mac said, "There you see, you understand. I can try but I still can't understand how you can just walk away from the season."

"Kid, lots of bad things happen at Christmas time. It's not supposed to either. It's supposed to be the time of year for 'good tidings to all.' On top of that, when you experience something bad, you look around and see the rest of the world happy and excited, celebrating a holiday that used to have meaning for you."

Mac looked at Paula with concern. "You had something bad happen to you one Christmas, didn't you?"

"Yes," she whispered.

"Then you should talk to her. Help her to understand that Christmas can still have meaning for her. Would you talk to her?"

"Whoa, whoa, whoa. Sounds like you want to help her with her problem more than just to get a photograph. That right, boss?"

Mac didn't want to deny it. His face changed from the competent, cosmopolitan man into a wide-eyed little boy. "I care about her, Paula. I want her to be happy."

Paula had wondered if she would ever see that look on Mac's face. It was the blossoming of love and she was surprised at the emotion she felt in seeing it. Although she loved Mac like a son, he could be a bit egotistical. Everything had always been about him, not the woman he was with.

Until now.

She gently patted his face and smiled. "Then we'll have to see what we can do."

The next day Mac called in to the diner and said that he couldn't work that day, not offering a reason why. He was polite on the phone, even friendly. Grace didn't know what to make of it.

By the afternoon, her nerves were on edge as she had her seventh cup of coffee. Her mind was tired from trying to say it didn't matter, then going to the extreme and agonizing over the thought of him leaving her to meet a girl.

When Ellen came in to take her shift, Grace was surprised to find Ellen just as agitated as she was. Mumbling under her breath, Ellen stomped back to the office to leave her purse and sweater, and then stomped back to the serving counter to pour herself a cup of coffee.

Thinking of her own day, Grace asked, "How many of those you had today?"

"I lost count."

It was almost funny that the two women did the same thing when bugged about something. In Grace's case it was a man. She wondered what Ellen could be . . . "What's going on with Howard?" Grace asked as she walked over to sit on a stool in front of Ellen.

"Nothing! Nothing's going on and nothing will ever be going on, ever again!" Again muttering under her breath, Ellen began adding teaspoons of sugar to her coffee.

Grace stopped her at five. Laying her hand across Ellen's coffee cup, Grace gently asked, "What happened, Ellen?"

Ellen's eyes began to water. She looked around to see if anyone was in listening distance. Big Jed and Little Jed were sitting on stools down from Grace. They nodded at her. Ellen leaned over and whispered in Grace's ear, "I think Howard's seeing someone behind my back."

"What!" Grace couldn't believe her ears. If anyone defined the word trustworthy, it was Mayor Howard Scott. "No, I don't believe it, you must be mistaken."

"Oh, so you're going to take his side?" Ellen said, not caring if the two Jeds heard anything.

Accustomed to Ellen's changing courses during a conversation, Grace tried to concentrate. "Of course not. Now, tell me what happened."

Taking a breath, Ellen said, "I caught him talking to some bimbo named Laura."

Thinking quickly, Grace said, "Well maybe it was a business call. Or maybe it was a family member."

Ellen shook her head. "He was too excited to be talking to her. How many people do you know are excited to talk to a family member?"

Grace thought about this. "Point taken. But how was he excited? What did he say?"

"He mostly listened. But he said . . . he said . . . 'How's my baby?'" The tears started falling from Ellen's face.

Grace walked around the counter and held her as she cried.

The Jeds were taking all this in with great interest. "You never know about them politicians. They seem all friendly on the outside but inside they're just waiting to stab you in the back," Big Jed said.

Rubbing Ellen's back, Grace said, "Please fellows. Not now."

"I know what you mean, Daddy," Little Jed continued not even acknowledging the two women. That senator from up North. Didn't they find out that he kept four different wives spread out over his home state? Maybe Mayor Scott has a whole harem, right here in Charity!"

Ellen cried harder as Grace gave the men a dirty look.

Tom came in from the kitchen where Bruiser stood by the sink peeling potatoes, intent on his work. Tom had heard all the crying and being a husband and father of five, two of them girls, thought he should see if he could help. He saw the two women, Ellen crying and Grace trying to soothe her. "What's wrong?"

"Ellen's upset because Mayor Scott has a bunch of women he's seeing, not just her," Big Jeb said.

Grace turned to him. "Will you stop that? Mayor Scott does not have a bunch of women. I'm sure there's a logical explanation for this."

"Yeah, Ellen. I've known Howard for years. He would never cheat," Tom said as he patted her back.

"Now, you see? Tom knows Howard wouldn't do anything to hurt you. Isn't that right, Tom?"

"Absolutely. And shame on you boys for putting such terrible ideas into Ellen's head," Tom added.

"Well, maybe we did jump to conclusions," Little Jed said.

"That's right," Grace said. "There's no proof of anything."

"After all, we haven't actually seen Mayor Scott with another woman."

"Of course you haven't," Grace said, rubbing Ellen's arm.

"Not like we seen Mac last night."

Everything in Grace froze. Slowly she turned her eyes to the two men and said, "You saw Mac with another woman last night?"

And just that quickly Ellen's tears were gone and she was reaching to steady Grace. "Grace, I'm sure they're mistaken. It's like you said, easily explained."

"Maybe so, Miss Ellen," Little Jed said. "But they were in the lobby of the hotel talking.

They kissed. Right on the lips. Then they went up in the elevator. Pretty little thing, too."

"I thought he looked too young for her, myself. Wouldn't mind having an introduction, though. Maybe she'd like to meet a nice older gentleman," Big Jed said smoothing out the thin strands of hair remaining on his nearly bald head.

If the situation hadn't been so confusing, Ellen would have laughed outright at that statement. But seeing Grace's pale face, she knew it wasn't funny. "Tom, would you get Grace a cup of hot tea. Decaffeinated."

"It's all right, Ellen. I'm fine."

"For heaven's sake, you're white as a sheet. And your arms are ice cold. Let me get something hot in you."

"No," Grace said in a small voice. So, she'd gotten her answer. Mac was with a woman last night. She should have guessed that she wouldn't have been able to hold his attention. She should have been thankful that the kissing hadn't gone any further the previous night, but right now she just wanted to get away. "Ah, I'm going to make the bank deposit and then go home." As if on autopilot, she walked to the cash register for her deposit. All eyes were on her. That is except for Bruiser who was still busy peeling potatoes. Her face and eyes were blank, as she put the deposit slip in a leather pouch.

Just then, the bell over the front door rang. Everyone looked to see who was coming in, Grace included. No one was more surprised than she was when in walked Mac—alone, but smiling from ear to ear.

CHAPTER NINE

The greeting that Mac received could have frozen an Eskimo. All eyes were on him with either confusion or anger. Except Grace's. He saw a look of hurt just before she dropped her eyes to her purse.

"Hey, everyone. What's going on?"

"Well, we were just sitting here wondering—" Big Jed started.

"Nothing," Ellen interrupted, giving Big Jed the eye. "Didn't expect to see you here today. I thought you were taking the day off."

"I am. But I had some unfinished business that I wanted to take care of." Then looking at Grace he said, "I was wondering if we could get together later. Maybe you could be my date for the big party in town tonight." For a second Mac felt like he was an actor in the role of "Biff" in some two-bit play about a small town in Arkansas. He never thought he would be uttering a sentence like that. But it was very important for Grace to be with him tonight. Maybe if she saw the season in the little town with him she would choose to embrace it once again. She was so close.

He also wanted her to meet Paula. Maybe Paula could talk with Grace and could impart some of her wisdom to her. Through the years Paula had become like a second mom to Mac. He wanted her to meet Grace, maybe in some way approve of her. It just seemed important to get her approval. Mac wasn't sure why.

"I've got plans. If you'll excuse me," Grace said coolly, not meeting his eyes. She briskly walked to the office. Ignoring the others, Mac followed, confused about her demeanor. Before he could get to the office, the door slammed, essentially in his face. Mac stood looking at it, his hands on his hips. He turned around and noticed that although everyone had been quietly watching, they suddenly had become very busy. Big Jed and Little Jed were both sipping their coffee and eating a slice of pie. Tom was checking the napkin holders to be sure they were filled. And Ellen was organizing the extra ketchup bottles on the shelf.

Something was up.

"So, anyone want to tell me why Grace is so upset with me?" Silence. "I sure would like to make it up to her, if I've done anything to upset her."

"You could dump your other girlfriend," said Little Jed before Ellen could hush him.

"Yeah, share the wealth. I'd like to meet her," Big Jed said. His hands went to adjust the collars of his shirt as if he were preparing for a date. "Perhaps she'd like to go out with a more mature man."

"My other girlfriend?" Mac was really confused now. But how was that new in this town? Sometimes he thought the locals fired on only half their cylinders. Mac thought hard about whom they thought might . . . "Are you talking about Paula?"

"So the tramp has a name?" Ellen said under her breath as she began organizing the mustards.

At that moment, Grace came out of the office and headed for the front door. Hoping to avoid a confrontation, she walked swiftly, keeping her head down.

"Grace, are you upset about Paula?" Mac asked.

Looking up, she saw that all eyes were on her. When did the sweet little town of Charity become another Peyton Place? She cleared her throat and said, "Of course not. Who you see is your business, not mine. Now I really need to get to the bank.

"Then you don't want to hear about my business partner getting in last night?"

Her hand on the doorknob, Grace stopped. She turned and looked at Mac. "Your business partner?"

"Yeah. Paula Tyler. My forty-eight year old business partner of six years."

"Yep, you got to watch those young women," Big Jed said.

Grace didn't hear him. Her eyes were fixed on Mac, who was grinning at her, apparently liking the fact that Grace was jealous.

"I knew she was coming but didn't know when she'd get here. When she called me last night I wanted to make sure that she was settled."

A frown came over Grace's face. Something didn't add up here. "What business, Mac?" she asked.

Oh gee! What should he say? "I call her my business partner," he stuttered. "She's a good friend. We've worked together in different towns, doing odd jobs for a while now. She helps me out sometimes."

"Taking pictures?" Grace asked.

Mac hesitated. "Sometimes."

With her eyes softening now, Grace said, "Why didn't you just tell me that last night?"

Mac looked around the room at the prying eyes and then walked closer to Grace and touched her arm. Quietly he said, "You had me a little worked up, honey. I couldn't think straight. All I knew was that we were interrupted and I didn't want to be."

The edges of Grace's mouth started to curve. The warmth of his touch began to spread throughout her body.

"Well, now that we got that figured out, why don't you two sit down and have a piece of pie. It's fresh pumpkin," Ellen said. Grace and Mac didn't move as the others began offering their own suggestions.

"Bring that friend of yours over for a bite to eat," Tom said.

"Yeah, she can sit next to me," Big Jed said.

"Daddy! You've got to play hard to get. That's the way women like it, don't you know," Little Jed added.

Big Jed snorted. "Yeah, look at all the ladies following you around."

Grace and Mac didn't hear any of them. They stood looking at each other as if no one else in the world existed.

An hour later the diner had begun to fill up with the early dinner crowd. Many locals wanted a bite to eat before setting up for the party and had heard that Tom was making his special Caribbean Christmas ham for dinner.

Ellen went back and forth from serving, bussing tables, and ringing up bills. Sally was on tonight. Bruiser was assisting Tom in the kitchen. As Ellen cleared another table and rushed to take the dirty dishes back, she saw the mayor come through the front door. She nearly dropped the bin. How dare he come in when she was too busy to let him have it!

Her head high, her shoulders back, she marched to the kitchen without a glance at the man standing by the checkout counter. Howard waited patiently by the cash register, knowing that she'd have to come there sooner or later.

They had been at lunch. His phone had rung and he went to the hallway near the bathrooms to take the call. When he got back to the table, Ellen was gone. A note scribbled on a napkin had simply said, "Go back to your baby." What was that all about? He had tried all afternoon, in between meetings and appointments to get in touch with her. All he'd gotten was voicemail. When he called the diner all he'd gotten was a dial tone in his ear.

Ellen was hurting for some reason and he was going to find out what that reason was. Even if he had to wait at the darn cash register all night!

A couple walked to the register to pay for their meal and Howard stood back smiling, waiting. Ellen rushed over.

"Everything all right for you two tonight?" she asked the couple.

With a verbal appreciation, a tip given to Ellen, and a smile between the two, the couple headed out the front door. Before Ellen could close the register and leave, Howard said, "Ellen," in that low, seductive way that he had.

"I can't talk now, Howard. I'm very busy," she said, trying to control her voice and her emotions.

He gently touched her arm. "Why did you leave me at lunch today? Did I do something wrong? I need to know?"

She guessed she owed him that. "I thought better of you, Howard. I thought you were a good man. Maybe uptight at times, but considering that you're a mayor and all, that's probably a good thing. But I thought you were a decent, honest man. It turns out . . . I was wrong." Ellen turned to leave, fighting back tears.

Howard tightened his grip on her arm. His mind was trying to block the different lines of thought she had just brought up and focus on the bottom line. "What's wrong? I walk away to simply take a call and then I come back and you're gone. What happened? And no more vague observations about my character, which we'll talk about later. What specifically has you upset?"

Ellen had initially liked that about Howard—he liked to cut to the chase to what was really going on. She knew that she had a tendency to go on and on, changing subjects as often as her mind did. But now, she found that trait a little embarrassing.

Before she could form a reply, someone stuck his head in the diner and said, "Mayor, they're waiting for you on the podium to start the party."

"I'll be right there, Ross." Then turning to Ellen he whispered in her ear, "I've thought about you all day. Please tell me what's wrong, baby."

That did it. All Ellen could think about was hearing the words "how's my baby" come from Howard to the mystery woman on the phone. Slowly, she slid her eyes up to his and in a low, menacing voice said, "I am not your baby. Perhaps you'd better go talk to your 'baby' on the phone again." And she jerked her arm away from his and walked out into the dining room.

Howard stood staring. A woman's mind had always been a puzzle to him, but Ellen's mind really took the prize. He'd never be able to figure her out. In a quiet voice Howard said, "What baby? The baby on the phone?" Then recognition registered on his face. A wide grin broke out as he realized what Ellen heard and must have thought. He couldn't have been more pleased. Up until that time he wondered if Ellen was as crazy about him as he was about her. Now he had his answer.

The annual town party always came the week before Christmas. It was filled with music, lights, treats, and something the people of Charity called "Florida Snow." It began with the closed street being sprayed with fluffy, white foam. Then at certain times during the evening, blowers connected to the light posts would blow out a mixture of soaps that appeared to be snow. All the children would go wild, running through the soap, making "snow angels" on the street. People strolled down the road as the speakers blared out a sentimental version of "White Christmas." Cameras would be flashing nonstop, hoping to capture a special image for the traditional family Christmas card. Who could resist? "Snow" in Florida! Mac had never seen anything like it in his life.

He and Grace had gotten a couple of slices of pizza from the pizza shop in town and were sitting watching the people when the first "snow" appeared. Mac grabbed his camera and walked out into the street to snap pictures. Grace watched him, amazed at his awareness of his surroundings and his instinctive knowledge of where to go for the best pictures. *He really should do this for a living*, she thought and determined to encourage him to market some of his pictures.

When the snow stopped, he walked back to their table, excited about the pictures he had taken. He clicked on the viewer and slipped his chair close to Grace's so they could view the pictures together.

Mac explained the way he framed the different pictures. Grace watched his eyes light up at the different shots. He was having a ball. Grace was more intrigued than ever by the man. Several shots she could just see framed in a home or business. Maybe even magazines would want Mac's pictures. A few of the pictures brought tears to her eyes as she saw her good friends, her neighbors, and her beloved children enjoying the season.

Showing Grace the pictures had first been an excuse to sit close to her. As he showed them to her, he realized how much he wanted her to like them. Her reaction floored him. She not only was interested, but seemed to have a good eye for detail as she made comments, listened to him explain what he was doing, and asked questions about why he did things the way he did. When she began to tear up over a few of the pictures, he knew that this was no ordinary woman.

He looked into her moist eyes and saw a woman that would interest him for the rest of his life. The whole idea struck him like a bolt of lightning. Without a thought, he leaned over and gave her a kiss. Grace looked at him and smiled.

They finished their pizza and grabbed a few cookies from the sweets table. Walking down the street, hand-in-hand, Grace asked, "Where's your friend? I thought I was going to meet her tonight."

"I don't know where she is. Probably enjoying the town," then looking down at Grace he added, "Like I am."

The music turned up loud again, signaling another round of snow coming. This time as the soapy flakes fell, Mac kept the camera on Grace. He snapped as she turned with her arms out, her head up, looking at the "snow." Mac captured the childlike joy in close-ups of her face, framed by falling snowflakes. Then Mac grabbed Grace around the waist and pulled her close. He angled the camera at them and took a series of shots of them enjoying the snow together. Before the snow ended, he kissed her tenderly, snapping away and hoping to get a nice shot of them together.

When the snow and music ended, Grace was still giggling. What a wonderful, silly, crazy thing—to be enjoying soapy snow in Florida just before Christmas.

She had never been happier in her life.

Paula had never seen a town like Charity. Most of her life had been spent in large towns, dealing with traffic, noise, and people. Lots of people.

As she walked through the sleepy town she soaked up the quiet contentment that she found. It seemed to pierce her heart and go right into her soul. She found herself sighing and smiling with each new sight. The houses were decorated simply and a delight to the eyes. On the hour, a nearby church would ring out the time. The chilly weather that was foreign to the South Florida resident didn't dampen her mood, but merely made her think of Christmas.

As she headed back to the downtown area, she could see all the people enjoying the evening. There were couples and families, children young and old all out talking and laughing with each other. It all looked so happy, so safe.

Safe. What a beautiful word. Paula took a deep breath and smiled. They couldn't know how good they had it.

As she stood looking, the "snow" started to fall. She laughed in amazement at these crazy Floridians enjoying the fake stuff. Paula started walking through the crowd looking for Mac and, she had to admit, enjoying the stuff herself. She liked this place. She liked this place a lot, could even consider spending some time here.

Paula spotted Mac right in the middle of the action. Naturally. She enjoyed seeing the wide smile on his face. It was so good to see her partner . . . happy? No, it wasn't just happiness. It was a joy mixed with contentment that she had never seen before. This girl must be something.

As Paula walked towards the middle of the street, her attention turned towards the girl that he was with. Mac was snapping pictures of her as she was enjoying the snow. Paula took a moment to study her. Not too tall, about the same height as her. Blonde hair cut just above the shoulders. The girl spun around and Paula watched her tilt her head back and laugh. Pretty smile. A dimple in her right cheek, how cute. It looked just like ... Paula stepped a little closer to get a better look but hid behind a group of people so as not to be seen by Mac. The big brown eyes, the slender nose, the high cheekbones. It couldn't be, it just couldn't. What had Mac said her name was? Her heart was pounding in her chest as she remembered that Mac had called her Grace.

She watched as the woman pushed her hair back with the flick of her wrist—a simple gesture that had Paula's whole world crashing down around her. Tears clouded her vision as she turned and sought an escape. She made it to the hotel and ran into the lobby, to the elevator. Her breath was coming in short gasps now. There was a pain in her chest as she tried to inhale. She knew if she didn't make it to her room quickly, she was liable to faint right where she stood.

Murmuring a quick prayer for help, the elevator doors opened. Paula jumped in and pressed her back against the side. As the doors closed she tried to take a few deep breaths, to get her composure back.

In her room, Paula felt sick to her stomach. She tried to calm down with a hot bath, an old movie, and a good book, but nothing could settle the tide of emotions swirling through her body.

Finally, she gave up trying. She took two sleeping pills and lay down in the darkened room. Outside, the party was still going on. She could hear cheers, chatter, laughter. Snuggling tighter under the covers, she tried to forget. Everything. Again, after a while she gave up trying. The sadness overwhelmed her and she cried bitter tears until the effect of the sleeping pills pulled her into oblivion.

CHAPTER TEN

The cheerful ringtone that meant Mac was calling her did little to brighten Paula's mood the next morning. She moaned as she reached for her cell. The headache that had been looming all night was in full force this morning so that when she answered the phone, her tone was biting.

"Wow! Rough night?" Mac asked with a touch of amusement. "What could you find to do in Charity that was so taxing?"

"Okay, smart alec. Give me a minute to take a couple of aspirin and I'll probably be able to converse with you," Paula said as she walked to the bathroom for the pills.

"I have a better idea," Mac said. "Why don't you come over to the diner and I'll set you up with the best coffee of your life. You know how much better you feel after you've had your morning joe."

Paula was instantly awake. "Thanks but I don't think so. I have some work I'd like to get done here first."

Mac laughed. "You're always working. Sounds like someone I know," he said as he cast a glance towards Grace. "Really. Just walk down the street to Hal's Place. You can meet everybody."

Hal's Place. Paula winced as she tried to think of a good enough excuse to get out of town. Fast. "No thanks, kid. I think I should probably head back to Miami Beach. I thought of a few things I wanted to take care of before Christmas."

Mac turned away from listening ears in the kitchen and quietly said, "Paula, what's wrong?"

How could Mac know that anything was wrong? "Nothing, nothing. I just think I need to . . . ah, do some paperwork on that Keys deal. It'll be here before you know it. We want to do a good job with that."

"You were supposed to meet us at the party last night. How come you never showed?"

"I was there. I spent yesterday afternoon walking around the town and ended up at the party. It was nice, sweet, very small towny." Was she babbling? She cringed knowing that Mac would know for sure that something was up.

And indeed he did. He also knew that Paula could be extremely secretive. He decided not to push it. "Listen, I'd like your help, and your eyes, for setting up a few shots I had in mind. I need you to stay for just a little while longer. Could you do that? Please?"

Paula had never been able to refuse Mac. Especially when he allowed himself to actually say "please." He had a boyish charm about him that reminded her so much about the only man she had ever loved.

And lost.

Sighing, Paula said, "Okay. But I still have some paperwork to do this morning. Tell me where you need me to meet you and I'll be there."

"Okay. Oh, and I'm going to bring along my assistant. Noel. He's a fifteen-year old kid that's helped me out a lot since I've been here."

"Sure, fine. No problem." Paula's heart started beating again. When Mac mentioned an assistant, she was scared about who he might have meant. She could meet a fifteen-year old kid, not a twenty-five year old woman. She had answers for that woman, answers to questions she wasn't even sure the woman wanted.

She wasn't sure she had the heart to tell her.

"Miss Grace, Miss Grace!" Holly came running into the diner, her cheeks rosy with excitement. "We're going to get our Christmas tree today!"

As she stood behind the cash register, Grace couldn't help but smile. The joy on Holly's face made her feel good. She didn't think about making excuses and dismissing the whole discussion that was about Christmas. She found that she wanted to stay and listen to Holly's excited chatter. "That's great, honey! Are you going to get a big one?"

"I don't know. My dad says we'll have to wait and see what they have left." Holly was almost vibrating with the thrill of being a child at Christmas. "Did you have fun at the Christmas party last night? We did! I ate about a thousand cookies and even made snow angels with my friends. It was like having a white Christmas, wasn't it?"

Laughing, Grace said, "Yes, it was. I enjoyed the party, too."

"I got two pennies." Holly pulled the coins out of her pocket. "Could I have two peppermints, please? One for my mama and one for me."

Holly was constantly coming in to buy something for her mother. "Your mom must have a real sweet tooth," Grace said as she reached for the candy. Then handing them over to Holly, she added, "Just like you."

Giggling, Holly said, "My daddy says me and Noel are just like my mama. He says we keep the dentist in business."

Grace chuckled. "Well, a little candy won't hurt you," Grace said leaning her elbows on the counter to give Holly her full attention.

Holly's face lit up. "You sound just like mama!" Then as if reciting a quotation that she'd heard many times over the years, Holly said, "Everything in moderation."

"That's exactly right."

"What's moderation?" Holly asked.

This little girl was too adorable. Grace walked around the counter and bent to speak eye-to-eye with Holly. Lovingly, Grace gently stroked the ponytail that hung down Grace's back. "Moderation is having a little bit of something every now and then. Just like candy, not having so much that you get a tummy ache."

"Oh," Holly said finally understanding the old saying. "Well, I'd better go. Thanks for the candy, Miss Grace." And with the speed of the young, she was gone.

Grace stood smiling after her when she felt a hand touch the small of her back. "Was that Holly?" the low, warm voice asked. Grace could feel herself weakening under the spell of it.

"Yes. She came in for some penny candy and to tell me that they were getting a Christmas tree today."

Mac walked to her side, still stroking her back. He had found that it was impossible to be near her and not touch her. He smiled down at Grace.

"What happened to your friend last night?" Grace asked. "I was looking forward to meeting her?"

"I'm not sure. Apparently she got so caught up in the town and the party that she went up to her hotel room exhausted." Deep down Mac didn't believe this but it's the story Paula gave so he'd go with it for now.

"That's a shame."

"Yeah. She wanted to head back down to Miami Beach but I talked her into staying for another couple of days. We'll probably leave together Christmas Eve." After he had spoken it, he stopped himself. It had always been in his plans to be back home in Miami Beach for Christmas. Now, Miami Beach seemed like the furthest thing from his mind. He didn't want to be anywhere without Grace.

Grace stiffened. She had forgotten. He was only here for a short time. He wasn't staying, she knew that. So why did the light seem to go out of her being at the thought of his leaving?

Both were quiet. At the tightness in Grace's face, Mac asked, "Are you okay Grace?"

"Yes, fine. Fine." Then gathering all her courage she said, "It's probably really nice right now in Miami Beach." Over the years Grace had learned how to mask a broken heart.

Mac looked into those big brown eyes and saw the hint of sadness behind the smile. Shrugging, he said, "It's okay." He wondered if Grace was thinking what he was thinking. He didn't really want to go. He would love nothing more than to share Christmas with her.

But that couldn't be for two, no, three reasons. First, Grace didn't celebrate Christmas. She would be in the diner, alone, all day. Maybe that's why he *should* stay. So she wouldn't be alone.

Second, Grace was heading to New York. She didn't want to be in Charity and had made it clear to him that she didn't want to be at Hal's too much longer. He could help her out with that. In fact, he had been thinking about it for a while now.

Third. He had to go back to Miami Beach. It was his home. He was ready to put down roots and Miami Beach had everything he wanted.

Except Grace.

He wouldn't spend the time they had remaining feeling sorry about the realities of life. He wanted to enjoy his time with this wonderful woman. "Let's go riding tonight, just around town. I want to show you the lights." Knowing that she could easily refuse anything relating to Christmas, he looked at her with a pouty expression. "Please?" Grace laughed, as he hoped she would. "You went to the Christmas party last night and had fun. How bad could it be to see a few beautiful lights?"

Leaning over to whisper in his ear, Grace said, "Well, as long as I'm with you it can't be bad."

Mac felt his blood heat. He wanted to take Grace to the office, close the door, and kiss her senseless. Instead he gave her a quick, tender kiss and said, "I'll pick you up at five-thirty."

Later when Ellen came into the diner, Grace could see that she had been crying. Her heart went out to Ellen but she felt she wasn't that much unlike her. Mac would be leaving soon and she would have to get on with her life.

Grace gave Ellen a hug and said, "Not a great night for sleeping, huh?"

Ellen sighed. "No." Then after putting her sweater and purse in the office she returned to Grace to say, "Howard came by last night."

"He did? What happened?"

Becoming furious again, Ellen said, "He acted like he hadn't done anything wrong, the jerk. He asked me to explain why I left the restaurant and left him alone. Like I did something wrong."

Ellen walked over to get a cup of coffee. Grace followed. "Did you ask him to explain himself?"

"I wasn't ready to hear any excuses." With a pained expression Ellen said, "I should just admit that this relationship isn't going to work out. I was so hopeful. He seemed like such a wonderful man." Grace wanted to say that she was sure he was, but from the look on Ellen's face, she knew the woman wouldn't hear her.

Ellen continued. "I think I'll just pack up and join some organization that needs help— maybe the Peace Corps or something. No, they'd have men there. Maybe there's a convent around that could use a restaurant hostess."

Trying to come back to the point, Grace poured herself a cup of coffee and said, "I don't think you should do anything drastic just yet, auntie."

With a smirk, Ellen looked at Grace. "You know how I hate it when you call me 'auntie.'"

"Yeah, I know. But it gets your attention." She smiled at the woman who had been her rock for the last ten years. She pulled Ellen to her and hugged her hard. "I love you, Ellen."

"I love you too, sweetheart."

Grace looked at Ellen and said, "Whatever happens, I'll still love you. *But* having said that, it wouldn't hurt to hear what Howard has to say in his defense."

Feeling like a silly clod, Ellen said, "I know. I was just so furious and so darn jealous that I wasn't thinking rationally." She sighed, resigned. "Now Howard knows what a flighty woman I am. So even if he has a good explanation, which is a big 'if,' he probably will not want to deal with a woman like me."

"He'd be blessed to deal with a woman like you. And I'll tell him so myself." Grace returned to her coffee, smiling at her aunt.

Switching tracks, as Ellen liked to do, she asked, "How was the party last night?"

"It was wonderful." A dreamy look came over Grace's face as she thought of the previous night. "We had pizza and cookies and played in the snow. Mac showed me the pictures that he took. He is really amazing, so talented. Later when most of the families had gone home, we stayed and danced in the snow while the music played. It was . . ." Grace couldn't find the right word. "It was . . . I mean Mac was . . . um, everything was great." She took another sip of coffee to hide her joy.

Ellen stood watching her, studying her, feeling a combination of happiness for the joy that her niece had found and dread for the pain that Grace would feel when Mac moved on.

When Ellen didn't say anything, Grace said, "What?"

As gently as a mother would, Ellen said, "Tell he how you feel about Mac, Grace."

A deep red blush crept up Grace's neck and covered her cheeks. She hadn't meant for this to happen, she really hadn't. But it had and she felt it necessary to share it with the closest person on the planet to her. Grace whispered, "I love him."

Ellen sighed deeply.

"No, it's okay, Ellen." Grace took Ellen's arm to reassure her. "I know it's not forever. I know that he's leaving. In fact, he told me this morning that he'll be leaving with Paula on Christmas Eve. I've decided to just enjoy the time that I have with him and when the time comes, we'll both go our separate ways."

Ellen stroked the hair away from Grace's eyes—the eyes that had shown so much sadness and hurt now showed a maturity that made Ellen proud. She smiled at Grace. "You are a special young woman. One day, a wonderful man is going to recognize that and sweep you off your feet. It's what you deserve."

I've already been swept off my feet, Grace wanted to say but didn't. "I don't know if I deserve it, but I'll enjoy it when the day comes."

In a low voice, Ellen said, "I really like Mac. I'm sorry it can't be him."

"Me, too. But life sometimes has it's own ideas."

She had no idea how right she was.

A cold front was forecasted to move in for a couple of days, making temperatures drop into the thirties. Before that happened, Grace enjoyed the feel of the wind as Mac's motorcycle carried them around the little town of Charity. By this time, Mac knew where all the most beautifully decorated houses were and he slowly drove by each one so Grace could get a good look. She "oohed" and "ahhed" over the displays that were lovingly put up by families in the town.

After showing Grace the town, Mac drove to a little park that was located on the other end of Main Street from the downtown area. They found a park bench and sat to take in the quiet of the evening.

Grace looked down the street at the businesses, all decorated in beautiful sparkling lights. Then she saw Hal's Place, smack dab in the middle with no lights, other than the utilitarian kind. For the first time ever, it bothered her.

Mac was sitting quietly next to her, his arm behind her, across the back of the bench. Grace turned to him and said, "You've stopped bugging me about putting Christmas lights up." Her eyes said it was more of a question than a statement.

"I decided that you had a good reason. Even though I can't fully understand it, it's yours and I respect that." Mac gave her a small smile. "And I hold out hope that you'll change your mind."

Chuckling, Grace said, "The eternal optimist."

"It's the only way to live, Grace," Mac said half joking, half serious.

Grace took a deep breath. "I wish I could live like that. But I can't . . . the past just somehow controls me. I can't forget."

"I don't think a person can forget." Mac hesitated. "But a person can choose to forgive."

"Forgive? Forgive?" Grace sat up straight and turned to face Mac squarely. "You want me to forgive the person that abandoned me? Who happened to be the most important person in my world?"

Mac took her hand and held it, rubbing his thumb over her fingers to calm her down. His other hand reached out and brought her back down against the bench and gently pulled her head to his shoulder. In a whisper he said, "Grace, no one's telling you what you should do. I hate should's. I'm not putting one on you now. I just mean that if you could try to forgive a little, your world wouldn't be so hard, so cold. So alone."

Grace thought about this as she enjoyed the feel of being close to him. With the complete honesty that Grace reserved for very few, she said, "Mac, I don't know if I can. I wouldn't even know how to start. How does a person get over that?"

"Hmm. Maybe the first place to start is Christmas." Grace squirmed a little. "Celebrating Christmas would be a very definite first step to forgiveness, don't you think?"

"Maybe." Grace was quiet for a moment and then said, "But I'm afraid that I've come to associate Christmas with . . . with death."

Mac looked down at her troubled face. "How so?"

"My mother left at Christmas, in essence dying in my mind. My father died at Christmas. To me Christmas is about death."

A sympathetic smile crossed Mac's face. "No, sweetheart. Christmas isn't about death. It's about a birth."

Grace thought about this as she again looked down Main Street to see the brightly decorated town.

And she thought about that birth in a quiet manger thousands of years ago and all the hope that came from that tiny baby.

"Hey, what are you doing hiding in here?" Mac asked as Paula let him into her room. "And don't tell me you're working. Even Trump takes a few hours off occasionally." Mac had dropped Grace off at the diner, given her a kiss, and headed back to the hotel to check on his partner.

"Very funny. I just thought I'd make an early night of it." They both walked over and sat in the chairs by the window.

Mac looked closely at Paula. The darkness under her eyes meant she wasn't sleeping. The puffiness meant she had been crying. "Paula, what's wrong?"

Seeing his observance of her eyes, Paula said, "Nothing! I'm just getting older. I need my sleep." Then trying to change the focus away from herself, she said, "You want something to drink? I've got some soda here and a few cookies, I think." She quickly jumped up and went in search of the items.

Knowing the maternal instincts of Paula to feed, Mac said, "Sure," allowing her time to compose herself. Whatever Paula was dealing with was definitely off limits to Mac. For now.

"So what are you working so hard on that you can't take some time off?"

"That Florida Keys layout." Paula sat back down, putting the cookies and soda on the table between them. "It's going to be a great one. Everyone seems to be bending over backwards to give the great photographer Stuart McCrae whatever he wants."

"I like to hear that!" Mac said. "It sure beats how hard we had to work at this six years ago."

Paula laughed. "You got that right. It's nice to have the other side get all the permits and permissions." She took a drink of her soda and said, "Listen, Stu. I thought I'd head back to Miami Beach tomorrow. I don't think I'm going to be any help for you here. That kid you got working with you is sharp."

"Yes, he is. How about staying a few more days. I'm leaving on Christmas Eve and I thought maybe we could follow each other back south."

Paula couldn't hide her surprise. "You're leaving so soon? You're giving up on your perfect photo?"

Running his fingers through his hair in frustration Mac said, "I've run out of ideas, Paula. I've tried pretty much everything I know. Tonight I thought I had her. We rode around town looking at lights and then sat in the park on the other end of Main Street." He sighed. "It was so evident that Hal's Place needed to be decorated. She understood that, I could see it in her eyes. She's so close. But she just can't take that last step."

The concern and love in Mac's eyes drew Paula's attention. "Sounds like you have feelings for this girl."

There was no use to hide it. Looking down at his soda, Mac said, "I do." Then shaking it off said, "But I hate to see anyone wasting a life in pain over the past."

"She has a lot to get over, Stu," Paula said quietly.

Mac looked up and narrowed his eyes. "How do you know what Grace has to get over?"

Paula took a breath and said, "Because I knew her mother."

CHAPTER ELEVEN

Eyes widened, Mac jumped out of his seat. "You knew her mother? You know what happened? That's great! Maybe you can talk to her, help her sort through this stuff, make her see that it's time to get over it."

"Whoa, whoa, whoa. I only said I knew her mother. I didn't say I was ever going to talk to her about it."

"Well, why the hell not! Maybe you can shed some light on why the woman took off in the first place. Help ease her mind that it wasn't her fault."

Appalled, Paula said, "Grace thinks it was her fault?"

"Come on, Paula. All kids think it's their fault when a parent leaves. I even thought it was my fault when my parents went traipsing all over the world. I thought it was because they didn't like me."

"You poor kid," Paula said.

Irritated, Mac said, "Don't feel sorry for me. That's what I used to think before Grandma set me straight. I had her to help me through it."

"Didn't Grace have her father?"

"Yeah, but from what she and Ellen tells me, Hal never really got over his wife just splitting."

Tears came into Paula's eyes. She blinked furiously to keep the invaders at bay. "Ellen, you said?"

"Uh-huh. That's Grace's aunt, Hal's sister. When they were having trouble getting on with their lives in Jacksonville, Hal decided to pack him and Grace up and move here with Ellen. He bought the diner and worked himself to death. Literally." Mac didn't notice Paula wiping her eyes. He reached for a cookie. "So, how did you know Grace's mother?"

Now looking up, he could see the tears streaming down her cheek. "Geez, Paula! What's the matter?"

Paula stood and began pacing back and forth. Finally she simply said, "Nothing." Then to answer his previous question, Paula said, "She was an old friend." Then reaching into the closet, she pulled out her suitcase and opened it on the bed. "Look, Stu, I think I'll just head back to Miami Beach tonight."

"Tonight?" Mac walked over to her. "Why?"

As she began putting her things into the case she said, "There's really no reason for me to be here. I think I should leave."

"But if you knew Grace's mother—"

"Believe me, I'm the last person that Grace would want to see. Now or ever."

"I don't understand. If you can help Grace, why won't you stay here and help her?"

Paula smiled sadly. "I think you can help her much better than I could. I could tell her things but I'm not quite sure she wants to hear them."

Mac took Paula's arms gently, stopping her from packing. "You know something about Grace's mother, don't you?"

Her eyes swimming in tears, Paula nodded.

Then because it was so like his nature, Mac enfolded her in his arms to comfort her. Mac could feel Paula shaking with her quiet sobs. *It must be a very sad story*, he thought.

Mac held Paula until she could get control of herself. Then with his arm around her, they sat on the edge of the bed.

"Paula. Whatever you know, I'm sure it's very hard to say." He rubbed her arm and gently said, "But don't you think it's time for the truth to come out? Don't you think Grace deserves to know what happened? She needs to know so she can put it away forever."

Mac smiled slightly. "Grace says that one of Ellen's favorite sayings is 'the truth will set you free.' I think it might just be what Grace needs." When Paula still didn't say anything, Mac continued. "Look at it this way. Of all the coincidences, you end up in the same small town as Grace. Maybe it's a sign that you're supposed to help Grace deal with this once and for all."

Sniffing, Paula shook her head. "It might just cause the hurt to surface again, Stu. I mean, her mother left. Without telling her goodbye, she left. How does a person get over that?"

The edges of Mac's mouth lifted. "Grace asked me that same question tonight."

"And what did you tell her?"

"Christmas."

When he didn't elaborate, Paula said, "Christmas? What do you mean?"

"Paula, Paula, Paula. You know how I feel about Christmas. There's a healing power to it. It's not just presents and trees and lights. It's what's behind all those things. The message of peace, hope. Love. It's a time to reach out, to forgive and ask forgiveness. It's a time of new beginnings."

Paula was taking all this to heart.

"Now, I don't know what you have to tell Grace, but I do know it's important for her to hear."

Paula trembled as she said, "I don't know if I can tell her."

Mac's arm tightened around her. "You don't have to be afraid. I'll be right there with you. And her." Then with a smug look on his face, said, "Stuart McCrae is an excellent multi-tasker. He can comfort two beautiful woman at the same time, no problem."

"Something to add to your list of skills," Paula said sarcastically. Then seriously she said, "I'll sleep on it, okay?"

It was as close to a yes as he was going to get tonight. He smiled at her.

"We need to add another case of ketchup to our next order. Boy, how do we go through so much ketchup?"

Not looking up from her paperwork, Grace said, "It's the Jeds. They like ketchup over their eggs at breakfast."

"Ewww! Who puts ketchup on their eggs?"

Grace smiled. Southern to the last inch of herself, Ellen couldn't see ruining a good fried egg with ketchup. "I guess some people like it."

The breakfast shift was over at the diner and Ellen had come in early to do some inventory. As she marked her clipboard, she said, "Well, some people are crazy."

"Indeed." Looking up, Grace took a chance and said, "Have you talked to Howard yet?"

Becoming extremely interested in her papers, Ellen mumbled, "No."

"Ellen! You can't let this thing go on. You need to clear the air." Grace got up from her desk and returned to the dining room to get it ready for lunch.

Ellen followed her. "I know. I'm just . . . you know . . ." Ellen stopped and sighed deeply. "I'm scared silly. What if he's moved on? What if he's not interested in making up?"

"Then he wasn't the man for you." Then having a brainstorm, Grace said, "And you call someone and make a date to prove that you're moving on."

Laughing, Ellen said, "Yes, I know just dozens of men waiting for my call."

"Don't worry. I'll find someone." Grace turned to Ellen and pointed her finger at her, saying, "But we are not going to let this get us down, no matter how it turns out, right?"

Ellen lifted a brow. "Since when did you become the adult and I become the child?"

"I prefer to think of both of us as adults. Competent, confident, wonderful adult women."

Ellen liked the sound of that. "That's right! You're absolutely right!"

Grace smiled at the light in her aunt's eyes. "All right, my fellow wonderful woman. Let's get back to work."

Three hours later, in the midst of the lunch rush, a frantic Mayor Howard Scott came bursting into the diner.

"Ellen!" he called. Not interested in the looks from customers enjoying their lunch, he stomped to the office calling for the woman.

Standing at a table, pad and pen in her hand ready to take an order, Grace's mouth dropped open. She had known Howard since she had moved to Charity. She had never seen him frazzled and disheveled.

She watched in amazement as he came storming out of the office, eyes scanning the dining room. When they landed on Grace, he stomped over to her, eyes blazing. "Where is she?"

Howard could make an intimidating figure when he chose to and at the moment, he chose to in a big way.

When all Grace could say was, "Ah," Howard scowled, "She's not at home so I know she must be here. Where are you hiding her?"

With wide eyes, Grace pointed back to the kitchen.

Howard turned and went to the kitchen, pushing the swinging door nearly off its hinges. By this point, all eyes in the restaurant where on the man. Mac put down his clean dishes to watch. Even Sal and Loretta had ceased their bickering to watch the scene play out.

Just as Howard was about to ask the cooks where she was, Ellen came out of the pantry. "Loretta, did you want me to order some more oregano?"

Ellen looked up, shocked at the silence. You could have heard a crumb drop. When her eyes met Howard's, she gasped. "What are you doing here?" she whispered.

"Enough games, Ellen. I've waited long enough for you to come to your senses and just plain out ask me about that phone call. Apparently, it's not an easy task for you to come to your senses." Offended by the remark, Ellen opened her mouth to reply. Her voice was cut off as Howard lifted his hand to silence her. "If you'd only taken a minute to ask me, I would have told you. I was speaking to my daughter-in-law."

Ellen snorted. "Yeah, right. Couldn't you come up with a better one than that? You don't have any children."

Howard sighed. "Yes, I do."

The silence got even quieter, if that was possible. All eyes and ears were trained on Howard as he started explaining.

"I was married, briefly, before I came to Charity. It didn't work out. As I was getting my life put back together, my former wife called me and told me she had given birth. The baby was mine." With a slightly bitter edge to his voice, he said, "I didn't know she was pregnant when I left. Anyway, when she called, she told me she had already found someone else and wanted to remarry. However, she felt I had the right to know that I was a father."

Ellen's eyes were filled with surprise and compassion as he continued. "After I met the new husband, I knew that it would be better if he functioned as father since he was right there and I wasn't. However, I visited every chance I got so that my son would know his real father." Taking a breath, Howard said, "Surprisingly it worked out well. His mother and stepfather did a wonderful job with him. He knew me, we spent time together not every week but often enough that he knew I loved him. He grew up into an incredibly thoughtful and intelligent man."

Blown away by the news Ellen let it soak in. Then with skeptical eyes she asked, "If you were talking to your 'daughter-in-law' why did you call her your baby?"

"Ellen, I wasn't talking about her. My son and his wife had a child, a daughter about six months ago. I was asking about my granddaughter!"

It made sense. Ellen thought that it made perfect sense that this caring man would ask about his baby granddaughter.

Now the time to eat crow had come. All eyes upon Ellen, she moved forward to stand in front of Howard. Clearing her throat and looking down she said, "I was going to ask you. I was just working up the courage to do it." Then with her large eyes looking up at him she said, "I'm sorry. Can you forgive me? Can you forgive my acting like a complete idiot?"

Howard couldn't wait any longer. He pulled her into his chest and hugged her tightly to the sighs of the women watching. Then unconcerned that there were others in the room, let alone the universe, Howard bent his head and kissed Ellen, firmly and hungrily on the lips.

Cheers and applause rang out all over the diner. Grace smiled with tears in her eyes. This was good. This was very good.

Her eyes met Mac's across the room. Their gaze held, as both Mac and Grace felt the same compassion, the same hunger.

The same love.

When the applause died down, things got back to normal at the diner. Howard took Ellen out for a late lunch, Mac took off for an hour, and Grace was left to finish waiting on tables—and thinking about what had just happened.

Howard and Ellen were good for each other. Ellen balanced out the stiffness of Howard, making him laugh and keeping him on his toes. Howard grounded Ellen and gave her the consideration, the love that she had missed in her life all these years. Grace could feel her throat clogging with tears thinking of the two of them together. With a stifled giggle, she wondered if she could give away the bride!

Too fast, there Grace, she thought to herself. Yes, they were a good pair but they were still getting to know each other. Could you really know that you loved with all your heart after being together for so short a period of time?

Yes! Her heart felt it. Her body confirmed it. Her mind reluctantly conceded to it. She felt that way about Mac. She didn't want to lose him. There were accounting firms in Miami Beach. Maybe she could . . .

But Mac hadn't asked her. And he likely wouldn't ask her. Mac had his own life in Miami Beach that he probably wanted to get back to. It didn't include her. They enjoyed spending time with each other, but come Christmas Eve he would be gone.

A spurt of anger came over Grace. How was she supposed to celebrate Christmas when everyone she had ever loved chose that time to leave her? Well, she was sick of it. Sick of it! Maybe it was time once and for all to take control of the situation. Maybe she should just talk to Mac about her moving to Miami Beach. What's the worst that could happen? He could say, "No. It's been fun, babe, but I'm moving on." Then what would she do? She could continue with her plans to move to New York City. Maybe hire someone to run the diner so she could just go.

But surely Mac would want her to come with him. The way that he held her in his arms, looked into her eyes had to mean that he had deep feelings for her. When they were near each other, they were always touching. Was he just going to leave that?

Maybe he was shy about relationships. Well, Grace could help him out with that. She would be patient and not expect everything at once. She just wanted to be near him in Miami Beach.

Now if only she could convince Mac that that's what he wanted.

She had to, that was all there was to it. She had to let him see how good they were together and know that she wouldn't mind following him south.

He didn't have to live the life of a drifter. His abilities with his camera could make a nice living. She could always get a job as an accountant. They could marry and maybe even have a child or two. Grace let a giggle slip out as she thought it through.

The power of her resolve started coursing through her veins. She was not going to be a whipping boy to fate any longer. She was in control now. As Grace picked up her tip from an empty table and began cleaning it, a smile of determination was on her face. She knew what she was going to do.

The wind started to kick up that afternoon, a sure sign that cold weather was on its way. Grace watched the wind swirl down the street, picking up a stray leaf or a piece of trash.

She could almost feel the cold biting into her flesh.

Grace sat at a stool working on the schedule for the next two weeks. She was going to get everything ready so she could leave for Miami Beach as soon as possible. Sal and Loretta were arguing about how many bay leaves to leave in the stew that they were putting together. Bruiser was nearby chopping vegetables for said stew. Tom was preparing a delicious carrot cake, chuckling at the quarreling couple.

In the dining room, Big Jed and Little Jed had their normal afternoon stools, eating slices of peanut butter pie and drinking coffee. The whole diner had a comfortable sort of murmur to it that put Grace at ease. And had her feeling a little sentimental.

No, no, no, she thought. She wasn't going to second guess her decision to leave with Mac. There would be no looking back, no tears, no guilt. Nothing! She had done what she felt she had to do, taking over for her father after he died. She had looked after her aunt, made sure she had everything she needed. Now Ellen had a good man that was crazy about her. Grace wasn't needed here. It was time to go.

Grace went back to work on the schedule when she heard the bell over the door ring. Looking up, she saw Ellen and Howard coming into the diner.

"I'm sorry I'm late. Howard and I lost track of the time," Ellen said as Howard helped her out of her jacket.

"No problem. It's been slow since the conclusion of our lunchtime show." Grace smiled mischievously.

Ellen walked to the office and Howard stepped towards Grace. "I'm sorry about that, Grace. I . . . went a little crazy. Your aunt does that to me."

"I know." Grace took a sip of her coffee, smiling. "It's adorable. And understandable. There's no need to apologize."

Looking around to see that Ellen was still in the office, Howard sat next to Grace and spoke softly. "I know that you're the only family that Ellen has nearby."

"That's right." Grace couldn't help but notice the vulnerable look in Howard's eyes. This was new. She had never known the mayor to be anything but his confident, strong self.

"I'd like . . . that is, I want . . . You see, it's this way . . ." The man was actually flustered. "Aw, hell. I love Ellen. I want to marry her. I hope you approve," Howard grumbled, trying to get the words out as fast as he could.

Grace laughed. Perfect, this was so perfect. She looked at the eager appearance of the mayor and could see the depth of love in his eyes. Not only had Ellen found a good man, she had found an adoring one. Then with a smile that threatened to split her face, Grace took Howard's face in her hands and kissed each cheek. "I approve," she said. Howard released a deep breath, causing Grace to giggle.

"When are you going to ask her?"

"I thought Christmas Day. She's making supper for me. Do you think she'll say yes?" His eyes pleaded for encouragement.

The humbleness of this man was unbelievable to Grace. She just wanted to cuddle him like she would a big, fluffy teddy bear. "I think she'll be thrilled!"

"She'll be thrilled about what?" Ellen asked entering the room.

"Oh, ah . . . ah . . . that Tom is making carrot cake. You love his carrot cake, don't you Ellen?" Grace asked trying to mask her happiness.

"Sure do. I can't wait." Then Ellen sighed as she put on her apron. "What can I get for you, honey? Coffee? Cake? Pie?"

Howard knew he had already gained a pound or two since dating Ellen so he said, "Just coffee, darlin'." And winked at her.

With a contented smile Ellen said, "Coming right up."

The phone ringing at the front counter had Grace hurrying over to answer it. As she picked up the receiver she thought, *yes, everything is working out perfectly*. Then seeing Mac coming through the front door, she thought, *absolutely perfect*.

Mac wasn't in the best of moods. For some strange reason, he felt a twinge of something between his shoulder blades. Now, he was not a superstitious man but every time in his life that he had gotten that twinge, something bad had happened. It was like a foreboding of something tragic.

He looked up at the diner and a warmth spread all through him. Strange to feel the ominous doom of something about to happen and at the same time feel a sense of contentment about where you were in life.

Maybe he was getting close to a nervous breakdown. His mind kept pulling him into different directions.

He still wanted that photograph. It was only a few days before Christmas and time was running out.

He knew something was up with Paula but she wasn't talking. She seemed to be distracted and short tempered. Maybe she just needed to get back to the beach.

And then there was Grace. The woman filled his every thought. Never before had he been so consumed with a female. It wasn't like him. It was stifling, it was confusing.

It was wonderful.

The thought of her blonde hair framing her face, the lingering scent of her sweet perfume, the big brown eyes that hypnotized him—his blood heated just in thinking about her. He wanted her, plain and simple. He wanted her body—that slim body that could set a fire inside of him just in being near. But it was more than that. He also wanted her mind. That sharp, logical, efficient mind fascinated him. He wanted her laugh. She had a laugh that took away any doubt that magic exists. He wanted to simply be near her, all day, everyday. Was that love? And if so, what was he supposed to do about it?

Walking into the diner and seeing Grace smile up at him, he decided. He was taking her with him. He had to have her. He would have a little explaining to do. All he'd have to say was, "Honey, I'm not a drifter. I'm a famous photographer." Surely that had to be okay with her.

Smiling, he walked over to her and kissed her lightly as she hung up the phone. Yes, everything was going to be okay.

Grace gathered up all her courage and said, "Mac have you got a minute? I'd like to talk to you in the office."

"Hey, Mac. We need you back here," Sal replied before Mac could answer.

He kissed her once more and said, "Yes. I need to talk to you, too. Let me take care of this first."

Howard watched this interaction as he and Ellen sat in a quiet booth sipping coffee. Turning to Ellen he asked, "Is that the young man you've been telling me about?"

"Yes. I'm sorry, I thought you'd met Mac," Ellen said.

Looking towards the kitchen, Howard said, "No, I haven't. Although he looks real familiar to me. Not sure why."

"Maybe it's because you saw him earlier in the kitchen, when we had our little . . . 'scene.'"

Howard chuckled. "No, that's not it. I've seen him somewhere else." Then he looked lovingly at Ellen and said, "Besides. I didn't notice anyone else in the world during our little scene except you." Howard lifted Ellen's hand and tenderly kissed it.

Ellen's sigh could be heard throughout the diner.

The door blew open and little Holly skipped up to the counter where Grace had returned to work. "Hi, Miss Grace."

Delight filled Grace as she looked down at the pink-cheeked girl. "Hi, Miss Holly."

Holly giggled at the greeting. "I'm supposed to wait for Noel here so he can walk me home." She climbed up onto a stool next to Grace and asked, "Watcha doing?"

"Oh, I'm making a schedule for everyone that works here so they'll know when to come and when to leave."

"Could I work here, too, Miss Grace?"

"Sure, when you get a little older," Grace automatically said. Then she remembered that she wasn't going to be here very much longer. To change the subject she said, "How about a glass of milk until Noel gets here?"

"Yes, thank you."

Grace poured the milk and placed it along with a sugar cookie in front of Holly."

"Oh, boy!" she exclaimed, as Grace chuckled.

Looking around at everyone in the diner, Grace got a funny feeling in her gut. Yes, she could admit to herself, she was going to miss Hal's Place and all the people that filled it.

"So what smells so good back there?" Howard asked as he sipped his coffee.

"I think the Spinuccis are making a beef stew," Ellen replied. "Hey Sal, how's the stew coming?"

Mac came back in from the alley in time to hear Sal ask, "What's that you say?"

Ellen pointed to the stove and said, "Stew."

"What?" Mac said turning toward the dining room thinking that someone was calling him. All eyes were on him. Realizing his mistake he said, "What . . . needs to be done in the dining room, Grace? Anything?"

Confused, Grace said, "You can bring out more glasses for the beverage stations." Lowering her voice a little she added, "Then we can have our talk." Mac smiled.

Everyone got back to what they were doing—Scheduling, cooking, chopping, eating, and chatting. Mac quickly got the clean glasses and began restocking the stations.

"My son and his wife invited me down for New Years Eve," Howard began. "I told them about you and they would like you to come with me. How about it?"

Ellen's first thought was that she absolutely wanted to go. Then looking at Grace bent over the schedule she said, "I'd like to, Howard. But Grace usually handles the diner on Christmas and I handle it on New Years Day."

Grace felt terrible. She couldn't let Ellen turn down a chance to meet Howard's family.

"Maybe we should just close down the diner for New Years Day," she said to Ellen.

A collective gasp was heard throughout the building. "Grace, you never close down for holidays," Ellen said.

"Well, maybe it's about time we did," she smiled at Ellen. Mac did a mental fist pump in the air. "I think you should go with Howard, get to know his family," Grace added.

Ellen's wide smile was worth more than any amount of money they could make in one day. "Thank you, sweetheart." Then turning back to Howard she asked, "Where does your son live?"

"A little town on the east coast. Stuart."

"Yes, what is it?" Mac straightened up to answer.

As everyone was quiet, pondering Mac's unusual entry into the conversation, Howard studied him. "Wait a minute. That's why you look so familiar to me. I know you. You're Stuart McCrae, the photographer!" Howard exclaimed.

Red faced, Mac tried to halt the discussion. Blowing out a puff of air he casually said, "Photographer? Why would you think I was a photographer?"

"I got your photos printed, Mac," Noel said as he entered the dining room. *What rotten timing*, Mac thought.

"Yes, you are, by gosh," Big Jed added, laughing. "I seen your picture on the back of your books. Never would have recognized you, though. We got your book about the nightlife of

New York City on the coffee table at home."
Howard raised an eyebrow at them.

"Hey, we might want to go to New York City one day," Little Jed said in his father's defense.

Looking back at Mac, Howard said, "I was at a fundraiser for the Handicapped Children's Aid in Tampa a couple of years ago. You were the featured speaker, and I must say you moved me to tears. Your books were displayed. I bought several of them."

Mac softly said, "Thank you," and sighed knowing that the jig was indeed up.

CHAPTER TWELVE

"Well, isn't this wonderful," Ellen said as she walked over and extended her hand to Mac as if meeting him for the first time. "It's so nice to meet a celebrity. And here in Charity at our little diner, of all places."

Both Jeds walked over to Mac and heartily shook his hand. The Spinuccis, Tom, and even Bruiser made their way over to Mac to pat him on the back or shake his hand. Noel and Holly looked at each other wondering what the big fuss was about. Even though the children knew of his books, he was just "Mac" to them.

Suspiciously quiet was Grace. She stood by her stool, arms folded across her chest with an unreadable expression on her face—unreadable except for her eyes. Mac kept glancing her way, trying to see how she was taking the news. He didn't like what he saw.

"What the Sam Hill are you doing in Charity, Mr. McCrae?" asked Little Jed. "If I was a famous photographer like you, I'd be in Africa taking pictures of cheetahs."

"Or in Hollywood taking pictures of movie stars," Big Jed added.

"No, he's probably here in Charity to get pictures of us," Tom said with a grin.

Loretta patted her face. "Well, it's a good thing I been using my wrinkle cream every night."

Sal studied her. "It's not working," he said and then, "Ow," as she punched his shoulder.

The excited chatter started again, louder this time, with Mac receiving more accolades and questions. Finally, Grace put her fingers in her mouth and whistled sharply causing a silence to descend over the diner.

"I'm sure that Mr. McCrae has a fascinating reason for being in Charity," she said slowly, enunciating each word.

"I'm here for the perfect Christmas photograph," Mac said without hesitating.

"Yeah, but that don't explain why you're here at Hal's bussing tables," Big Jed said. Everyone waited for Mac's answer.

"I think I understand," Grace said, a frigid tone in her voice. The diner got very quiet. Tension crept into the room. A tight smile formed on Grace's face as she said in an overly polite, low voice, "The perfect Christmas photograph, what a charming idea." The expression on her face was deceiving to the casual eye but those in the diner knew. Little Holly stood behind Noel. Ellen's eyes grew wide. Howard held his breath.

"I've never seen her so mad before," Little Jed said.

"But you're having trouble getting it, aren't you?" Grace said, keeping the same expression.

"It's downright frightening," Big Jed said.

"Too bad your little plan didn't work."

"It's not over until it's over," Mac simply replied, not yielding to the sharpness of her tone.

His eyes were sharp and intent, waiting to see how this played out.

"Of course." Then taking a shallow breath Grace said, "We hope our little town has given you a lot of . . . great photographs. But now . . ."

In a stage whisper, Big Jed said, "She's gonna blow!"

"If you'll excuse me." And then Grace briskly walked back to the office and closed the door.

The silence in the dining room was deafening. The atmosphere felt like a big balloon had been deflated. No one knew what to say. Finally, Mac said, "I ah, think I'd better go talk to her."

"I think you should," Ellen said. She was concerned about her niece but at the same time wasn't foolish enough to approach her at that moment. Mac, however, deserved to experience Grace's wrath for the hurt that Ellen knew vibrated behind her phony smile.

Without knocking on the door, Mac went in and found Grace on the phone. "How much do you think we need to lower the price, Valerie? You could say that the owner is very motivated."

"Grace," Mac said.

She held up a hand to silence him. "Yes, yes. That's fine. I'd like to hear something in the next two weeks. I'll email you my forwarding address for all the paperwork."

As she hung up and flipped through a notebook, Mac said, "Grace, we need to talk."

Finding a phone number, she punched it in and waited. "I'm rather busy right now." After a connection was made, Grace said, "Hello. I'm calling to schedule an interview for the position in the accounting department that you posted." Mac took a seat while Grace continued her call. He was not leaving until they talked. "Not until after the first?" Grace was annoyed and rolled her eyes. "Yes, yes, I know it's Christmas. All right when can you schedule me?" Writing down in the notebook and giving her contact information, Grace politely ended the call. "Really, Mac. I mean, Mr. McCrae. I've got a lot to do right now. I'm sure you're busy as well."

Mac turned to look at her computer screen. She had a travel site up, booking a flight to New York for the next day. Looking at the prices, Mac whistled. "You're going to get clobbered by the costs of flying right now. Might as well wait until after Christmas."

Looking through the few available flights, Grace said, "Thanks for your advice but it doesn't concern you."

The hurt in her eyes was a telling sign. Her beautiful eyes that always displayed her emotions—determination, joy, annoyance, passion. Now they spoke of disappointment and an emotion that tore at Mac's heart—loneliness.

"Grace, you have every reason in the world to be angry."

"I'm not angry," she said still clicking on the site.

"Look me in the eye and tell me you're not angry," Mac said with frustration.

"I really need to get this done so—Hey!" Mac reached over and clicked off the Internet access, causing Grace to swirl in her chair and face him.

"Good. Not you'll talk to me."

"Listen, Mr. McCrae—"

"Cut the 'Mr. McCrae' crap. I'm still Mac. I'm still the same man that I was twenty minutes ago before you found out my whole damn name."

Grace leaned back in her chair and folded her arms. Looking into Mac's eyes she said, "Okay, you want to talk? We'll talk. How about we start by how you lied to me by letting me think you were just some guy down on his luck. I'm sure you had a good laugh over that. But let's see, why would you actually take the job of busboy here at the diner? What would make a famous photographer agree to work for minimum wage in a two-bit diner in Nowhere, U.S.A.?" Grace snapped her fingers for effect. "Oh, I've got it. It had something to do with that picture, of course. Maybe the owner of the crackerjack diner wouldn't put up decorations and you decided, persuasive guy that you are, that you would stay close to that owner and somehow convince her to put up Christmas decorations for an award-winning photograph to go along with an award-winning life. Am I getting close?" Grace mocked.

Mac could feel the heat creep up his neck. "Essentially. In the beginning it was like that," he admitted.

"But she just wouldn't crack, would she, Stuart McCrae?" Grace laughed without humor. "I've got to say, you were good. You had me completely fooled. That's not a small task. But you really went far and above the call of duty. What were you going to try next? Seduce me? Get me into your bed hoping to change my mind?" Grace clucked her tongue. "Shame on you, Stuart McCrae."

"Grace," Mac pleaded. "It wasn't like that. I care for you, you must know that."

Mac saw a flicker of emotion pass through Grace's eyes. Then a steely determination came as she looked back at her desk. "Well, whatever we had was nice, but it's over. I have a life to live, as you do as well."

Sighing Mac said, "If that's the way you want it." It wasn't what Mac wanted but he knew Grace was too angry right now to think straight. He'd give her time to cool off and then he'd be back with a vengeance. Perhaps now would be a good time to play his trump card. "But before I leave the office, I'd like to make a business proposition."

How dare him! The way he just let go of their relationship was very telling. Apparently it hadn't meant the same to him that it had to her. She had to get out, get away as fast as she could. Looking back at her computer, she said, "I don't believe there's any business that I'd like to conduct with you."

"I'd like to buy the diner."

Grace was too stunned to utter a reply at first. She looked back at him with her eyes narrowing and muttered, "Buy the diner." She took a deep breath. "Well, that was one scheme I didn't see coming. So, we're into bribery now, are we?"

Not taking the bait, Mac said, "What do you say?"

Not trusting him, Grace asked, "Why?"

"I have my reasons. The perfect photograph, remember? Besides, what does it matter? I'll pay your full asking price. Everyone can stay on here. If Ellen wants, she can manage the place. If not, I'll get someone else."

He was giving her a way out, a way to go to New York free and clear. Free and clear of him, also. "Interesting," she said as she thought about the offer.

"I only ask that you wait until after Christmas to leave?"

Suspicious, she again asked, "Why?"

Mac wasn't quite sure why it was important; he just knew that it was. "Because I'd like you to be with your family for this last Christmas before you move to New York. Even if it isn't important to you, I know it is to Ellen."

The guilt card. *No fair*, Grace thought. "I also have one stipulation on the deal. You won't put up Christmas decorations until I leave."

Mac thought it through. He stood and stretched out his hand. "Deal."

Grace stood also. She joined her hand with his and said, "Deal."

Both were getting what they wanted. So why did they both feel so empty?

News of the impending sale of the diner to the award-winning photographer Stuart "Mac" McCrae flew through the town faster than Santa on Christmas Eve. Everyone was stopping by the diner to congratulate Grace on the sale and to wish her the best. She graciously accepted their wishes with a smile—a smile that covered her heartbreak.

Mac had left the diner after his deal with Grace to call his attorney and get the ball rolling. After explaining everything to Paula, they took her car to the local super mart to load up on more Christmas decorations to add to the stash hidden in the diner's large pantry. If he was going to be able to decorate any way he pleased, he was going to make Hal's Place a showplace for Christmas aficionados.

Just as soon as Grace left.

Of course that meant staying in Charity through Christmas, but Mac wanted to get decorations up, even if it was for the week after Christmas. Maybe he could get a few shots to use for next year. Besides, the town would probably enjoy the sight. And he needed to stay in town to close the deal transferring ownership of the diner. He couldn't leave before . . .

Honestly, he just didn't want to leave the little town.

As Paula drove back to Charity, the car loaded with purchases, she glanced at Mac sitting quietly beside her, deep in thought. He wiped his hand over his face and let out a deep sigh.

"Everything okay, Stu?"

"Huh? Yeah. Couldn't be better," Mac replied quietly.

"Well, it looks like you're finally going to get your photo after all. I knew you could do it," Paula said in a chipper voice.

"Hmm," was Mac's reply.

"How about we celebrate tonight? I heard there's a wonderful French restaurant just up the way in Orlando. It'll be my treat."

"I don't think so. I was thinking about looking over your information on the Keys project and then hitting the sack. Thanks anyway."

This was not right. The Stuart McCrae that Paula knew would never say no to a French dinner. It was obvious to Paula that Mac was brooding over Grace. On the one hand, she should be very happy. Their parting meant that he wouldn't pressure her to have a talk with Grace about her mother. On the other hand, Paula hated to see her good friend so depressed.

Mac typically didn't discuss his women with Paula. She never asked. This time was different. Knowing that she would have to handle the situation delicately, she said, "So, Grace is leaving the day after Christmas?"

"Yeah, that's right," Mac muttered.

"She's heading to New York?"

"Uh-huh." Mac put his elbow on the car door and with his head in his hand looked at the passing scenery. Paula's heart went out to him. He looked like a dejected little boy who was told that Christmas was cancelled.

Paula said quietly, "You do know that it's probably better this way. I mean with you and Grace."

This got Mac's attention. Turning to look at Paula he said, "How do you figure?"

"Stu. You both want different things. You want to plant roots in Miami Beach, take your pictures, and play in the sun. She wants the big city, a career, life on the fast track."

Mac thought about this. "I guess. I just thought . . ."

"Yes?"

"Nothing," Mac said shaking his head.

Paula couldn't let things stay this way. With a serious face she said, "It's for the best. From what you've told me, she really wasn't your type at all."

"Oh, come on Paula. You never even met her," Mac said feeling the need to defend Grace.

"True, but what kind of a life would you have with a woman like Grace. From the way you tell it, she's opinionated, stubborn, obsessively neat and organized. Nothing like you, Junior."

Mac smiled at the thought of Grace. "Nothing like me."

"And she hates Christmas! What in the world would you do with a woman that hated Christmas? And if the two of you had children, how would you deal with the holidays? It's always been a very special time of the year for you."

Still smiling, Mac said, "She was coming around."

"Maybe. Still, with all you've told me about her, I think you had a close call, buddy. And even though you said she was generous, caring, intelligent, beautiful even, the last thing you want is to be trapped in a marriage with a woman like her." The idea had been sounding better and better to Mac.

Until he went and ruined it.

Mac looked into Paula's serious brown eyes. He loved Paula just like an older sister, or a surrogate mother. Right now, he could see right through her. He reached over and squeezed her hand. "Paula, you're the best friend I have. I know what you're trying to do. You're trying to get me to admit my feelings for Grace, but you don't have to. I know how I feel. I know what she is to me. Unfortunately, I don't think she'll forgive me for not telling her who I am."

Paula was suddenly filled with irritation. "What's the matter with that girl. Doesn't she realize the very meaning of her name? Isn't she supposed to be full of mercy and pardon? Instead all she does is hold grudges and festers old wounds."

"Don't be so hard on her, Paula. I'm sure when the time comes, she'll deal with what she needs to deal with."

Paula thought about this. She knew what she had to do. She knew the time had come. Her body began to shake just thinking about it. But she loved Mac and knew he was right about Grace. Paula wanted to help the girl and she was the one to do it.

"Stu?" she said with a quiver in her voice.

"Yeah?"

With a deep breath Paula said, "I've decided to tell Grace about her mother." Mac's eyes widened. "But I first want you to know that it could go one of two ways. Best case scenario, it could help heal the hurt she feels."

When Paula hesitated, Mac said, "And what's the worst case scenario?"

Stopped at a traffic light, Paula looked straight into Mac's blue eyes. "She might never want to have anything to do with either one of us again."

The cold front that had been promised finally hit. Grace and Ellen were kept busy serving coffee and hot chocolate to the Floridians who just didn't know how to dress for cold weather. The wind kept curling off the lake to wrap around the little diner, emitting a low howl that sounded like a distress call.

Grace tried to keep busy, thinking of leaving for New York in a couple of days. There was so much to do—packing, turning off utilities, using up food. Annoyance had plagued her as so many companies were in holiday mode and not interested in accommodating her timetable. Children from Charity had been by since the night before, hugging her and telling her how much they would miss her. Ellen would look at her and begin crying. How much could she take?

All forces seemed to be against her leaving, but she determined that wouldn't stop her.

During a lull in the afternoon, Paula's car pulled up to the service area beside the diner. Grace was busy in the dining room and didn't notice Mac and Paula coming in the back door, carrying in box after box of Christmas decorations, storing them in the pantry.

When that was done, Mac wiped his hands on his jeans and said, "Are you ready?"

Paula was literally shaking. Her eyes showed a torment that pierced Mac's soul. He quickly took her in his arms and said, "Paula. It'll be okay."

A sob rose from Paula's throat and escaped against Mac's shirt. "I'm scared, Stu," she whispered.

"I'll be right there with you. It'll be okay." Then sensing that she was getting control back, Mac eased away from her and took her hand. Squeezing it, he smiled and said, "We'll do this together. It's for Grace, remember?"

"Yes." Her watery eyes looked at him. "Promise you won't hate me?"

Mac thought it a strange request. "Darlin', I could never hate you. Whatever it is you have to tell Grace, I'll stand with you. I promise." He kissed her hand.

Paula tried to give him a small smile. He put his arm around her shoulder and led her out of the pantry.

The kitchen was peaceful as the cooks were quietly working. They gave a nod to Mac and looked questioningly at Paula.

"Everyone, this is my business partner, Paula Tyler. You'll probably be seeing her around a lot as we get everything settled here."

After the individual introductions, Paula stood back to look at the kitchen. Very nice. Very efficient. She would have expected nothing less.

As Loretta began to ask Paula a question about herself, Grace came in from the dining room.

"Tom, have we got any—"

Looking at Mac and Paula standing there, every bone in Grace's body froze. Not only froze, they hardened, making moving an impossibility. Her eyes were unusually wide, her mouth hanging open; if the situation were different, Mac would have compared her reaction to a Looney Tunes cartoon character. Her eyes showed disbelief so powerful, Mac would have thought she had seen a ghost. After a moment, the eyes turned bitter and hard, and so cold that Mac felt he needed an extra jacket on.

"Hello, Grace," Paula said in a small voice.

With her little remaining strength, Grace summoned up the ability to utter a single coherent thought.

"Hello . . . Mother."

CHAPTER THIRTEEN

"Mother? Did she just say mother?" Mac asked those in the room who looked as confused as he. Then as Grace and Paula just stood looking at each other he said, "Paula, did she just call you mother?"

Not taking her eyes off Grace, Paula's lips curled slightly. "Yes, she did. I'm her mother, Stu."

Mac felt like he'd just taken a punch in the gut. "What do you mean, you're her mother?" he asked, his voice rising.

"Ten years ago, I left my husband and daughter. I'm sure she told you about it."

Grace's furious eyes hadn't left Paula. The hurt was so intense it threatened to make her physically ill. The only way she could stand still was the anger that gave her legs strength.

"Grace, what happened to you?" Ellen asked as she entered the kitchen. When she saw Paula, her eyes got as big as saucers. "Oh, my! Pauline, is it you?"

"Yes, it's me. How are you, Ellen?" Paula asked kindly.

"What the hell is this, McCrae, some sick joke?" Grace turned to look at Mac. "You got your diner to decorate anyway you want. You want to completely destroy me now?"

"Of course not!" Mac replied.

"Where did you find her? Was it hard? Let me guess, maybe a bar in Jersey City or a brothel in Nevada?" Paula's eyes filled with tears.

"Grace! That's enough!" Ellen walked over to gently hold onto Grace. She noticed that her niece was standing too still. Ellen was afraid that she would fall over at any minute.

With venom in her voice Grace shouted, "I want her out of my diner right now!"

"It's my diner now," Mac challenged.

"Not yet! I still run things until the papers are signed and I want this . . . this," Grace couldn't think of a bad enough word to call Paula. "I don't even know who the hell this person is."

Coming to Paula's defense Mac put his hands on her shoulders. "This is my business partner, Grace, Paula Tyler. She's been working with me for six years now." Mac was at a loss. What should he do? "I had no idea she was your mother. I know there are issues to deal with here, questions to be answered, but I also know that Paula is a kind and thoughtful human being."

"Sure! That's right. Unless you happen to be her own flesh and blood. Then she couldn't care less."

"That's not true," Paula said quietly. As Grace's eyes shot arrows, Paula began to speak. "There was a reason for my leaving."

Still firmly being held by Ellen, Grace folded her arms and said, "Well, I can't wait to hear this one." When Paula hesitated, Grace said, "Go ahead."

Noticing everyone in the diner watching the conversation, Mac said, "Maybe we should take this into the office." Then he took Paula's arm and gently led her away. It galled Grace that Mac would be so caring, so gentle with the enemy. She didn't want to hear any excuses for why she was abandoned. It would probably be a pack of lies, anyway. Everything she had ever told Grace was a lie—including that she would always love her. A lie.

Now, here she was going to explain ten years away, ten years that Grace had suffered knowing that her mother didn't love her. As they were walking by the front door of the diner, Grace had an immediate urge to jet out the door and hide until her flight to New York. She did not want to face this woman, opening the pain that occurred ten years ago. Ellen's gentle but firm hand on her shoulder told her that she had no choice.

Once inside the office, Ellen directed Grace to her chair behind the desk. Mac helped Paula into the folding chair. Then with the look of sports umpires, Ellen and Mac stepped back to watch the proceedings.

"All right, mother dearest. We have privacy. Would you like to now unburden your soul and dump all your garbage on me?" Grace mocked.

Paula's eyes grew sharp. "No! That's exactly what I wanted to avoid since the day you were born. I didn't want any of the ugliness of my former life to affect you or your father."

"Former life? I suppose you're going to tell me you're some kind of a spy. You left because you were on a mission." Grace laughed harshly.

"No, it wasn't anything so noble as that," Paula muttered. Looking up into her daughter's eyes she saw her beloved Hal. It hurt her heart but she knew she had to keep going, for him, for Grace, for her. "Grace, a long time ago, before I met your father, I was a very wild kid. I turned into a wild adult who got mixed up with some very bad people." Paula could see the disbelief on Grace's face but she continued. "The men that I hung out with were pretty rough. They were in . . . let's just say some very bad and very illegal things.

"One day I took a look at my life and realized what a horrible mess I had made of it. In the middle of the night, I took off for Florida. I wanted to get as far away from them as possible." A gentle smile touched Paula's face, causing her to appear as a young girl. "Then I met your father. He was so kind and so loving. He was a hard worker, a good man. I fell instantly and completely in love with him. Before I knew it, we were married and you were on the way. I was the happiest woman in the world.

"I loved being a wife and a mother." Grace tried to scoff at that but she found that a lump had formed in her throat and all she could do was listen. "You were the apple of my eye. I loved brushing your hair and braiding it. I loved making picnic lunches and going with you and your father over to Trout River to watch the fishermen and to play with you on the playground. Do you remember that?" Grace looked down, unable to answer. "I especially loved Christmas. It was always better through your eyes, Grace. I remember you loved the song 'Away in a Manger.'" Paula chuckled. "I had to sing it to you every night before you'd go to bed." Tears were creeping down Grace's face silently.

Then a sadness crept into Paula, a deep, bone-weary misery that instantly aged her. "Everything was fine for years. There was really no reason for anyone to pursue me. Then my 'former associates' were arrested and a court case was built around them." Paula sighed deeply. "I knew things, Grace. Bad things about them. I was a loose end that needed to be tied up. They put out a contract on me." Ellen and Mac gasped. Grace frowned trying not to show Paula any sympathy.

Paula looked Grace in the eyes. "A friend managed to get word to me that they were heading to Florida to find me. I had to get away before they found you and your father. I couldn't risk your being hurt because of me."

The irony of the statement wasn't lost on Grace. She smirked. "So let me get this straight. You left so that I *wouldn't* be hurt?"

"I left so you wouldn't be *killed*! Grace, those men were killers. I'd seen them kill before. They had no soul, they'd just as soon use a kitchen knife and cut out a heart as say hello." Tears started to pour down Paula's face. "Don't you see I had to leave so that you would be safe?

You were my baby, my precious child. I . . . couldn't let . . . anything happen to you!" Her sobs were deep and gut wrenching. Grace's tears were flowing as well. "I'll always love you, Grace," Paula whimpered.

Grace's eyes shot up. She started trembling with fury, emotion, and hurt. "You don't know the meaning of the word love!" Her voice shaking, Grace continued. "How can a mother abandon her child if she loves her? If what you say is true, and I'm not sure that it is, you could have taken us with you. We all could have left together. But no! You abandoned us!

"I went for years crying every night over the fact that my mother didn't love me, that she cared so little about my father and me that she took off. Do you know what it's like to become a woman and not have your mother to talk with you about it, but knowing that she's somewhere out there making a life without you?"

With cold eyes Grace said, "And you can't possibly know how it feels to watch the person you love work himself into an early grave over losing his wife. I watched all that happened, I lived it. I loved Daddy to the end. I was there because you weren't so don't walk in here and tell me about love!"

Paula was retching with grief as Grace stood and headed for the door. Mac blocked it as Ellen took Grace's arm. As kindly as she could, Ellen said, "Grace. Don't leave, not yet. This hasn't solved anything."

Vibrating with emotion now, Grace shook off her aunt's hand. "I don't want to hear it. If she wants to give excuses, you're welcome to stay. I've had enough." Then eyes spitting fire, she turned to Mac. "Get out of my way, Mr. Whoever the hell you are. You both deserve each other."

With a look of resignation, Mac moved away and let Grace leave. Ellen went over to the weeping woman and knelt. She put her arms around Paula and hugged her tightly. Deeply touched by the Ellen's gesture, Paula clung to her. "I loved him, Ellen, I loved him so much."

Ellen rocked her and said softly, "Of course you did."

"And Grace. I love her. I'd never have left if I thought there was another way. She was my life, my heart and soul. She doesn't understand."

"I know, I know." Ellen continued to rock and comfort Paula.

Mac watched as Paula wept for the years she had lost with her family. He marveled at the compassion that Hal's sister showed. With fury he thought it should have been Hal's daughter.

His breath coming in quick fits, he walked over to the women and knelt down on the other side of Paula. His hand went to her shoulder and gently caressed. This woman was so special to him and it hurt him to the core to see the anguish she was in.

All because of the woman he was in love with. What a crazy, mixed up world it was.

As Paula continued to weep in Ellen's arms, Mac said to Ellen, "Would you stay with her until I get back? I have to . . . do something."

"Yes, I'll stay with her." Then with understanding in her eyes she said, "Mac. Grace is hurting, too. Remember that. Don't go too hard on her."

Mac smiled sadly at Ellen. She knew exactly what Mac was going to do—try to help Grace through this.

As he left the room, Ellen said a quick prayer for Mac. He was going to need it.

Grace ran back to her apartment. She quickly changed into running gear and headed for her favorite jogging trail. She had to run. She had to sweat. She had to get all this garbage out of her system or she was going to detonate.

The first mile came and went without her even feeling her legs. The pain that hammered at her system was unlike any she'd ever felt. It was more acute, more intense than the pain ten years ago when her mother left.

She told a good story—she left so her family would be safe. It sounded good, very righteous. Was it true? It didn't matter. She'd been gone for ten long years. It was only fate that had her mother back in her life. Pure, despicable fate.

Her pace picked up again along with her breathing. The frigid air did nothing to hamper her stride.

"What's your hurry?"

Grace turned to see a man sitting on a bench. Déjà vu was her first thought, as she walked back to face Mac. It was the bench she had found him at his first morning in Celebration.

But Grace had no patience for fond remembrances just now. "So, you make a fool of me, stab me in the heart. What did you come out here for, hope to finish me off? So much for your Christmas spirit."

"Grace, I know you're furious, you're reeling—"

"You don't know the half of it, buddy. I can't believe that I actually had feelings for you. You throw my worst nightmare right in my face without the least bit of consideration for me."

"You've got to believe me when I tell you I didn't know Paula was your mom," Mac said.

"Pauline! Her name is Pauline Hudson, the estranged wife of Hal, absent mother of Grace." She began pacing in front of him, fists at her sides. "How could you not know her real name?"

Mac leaned forward, his elbows on his knees as he sat on the bench. "Years ago, a woman answered an ad I had placed for an assistant. She told me her name was Paula Tyler."

"Hummph. She got the Tyler from her hometown. Tyler, Texas."

"I guess. Anyway, she was such a hardworking employee, she never gave me any reason to suggest she was hiding anything."

"Now she's your partner?"

"Yes, she deserved it." He paused and then said, "She had no idea you were here. When she found out who you were, she told me she knew your mother. That's why I brought her to the diner today. I thought maybe she could tell you things you needed to know."

Grace looked into Mac's eyes—eyes so blue it made her want to curl up in them and cry her heart out. She believed he was telling the truth. But she had to hold onto her sense of justice here. Mac and her mother had both lied before and they would do it to her again if she gave them a chance.

"You lied to me about who you were," Grace mumbled. It still hurt her to know that Mac hadn't told her who he was.

"I didn't lie. I never lied. I just let you believed what you wanted to. Grace, honey, what would you have done if I had come in the diner, told you who I was, and asked you to decorate so I could get my picture?"

"I would have told you to take a hike," she admitted.

Mac snorted, "Probably in more graphic terms. I never lied to you or set out to hurt you in anyway, you've got to believe me.

Grace paused and thought. "Okay, I believe you. Was that all?" she asked backing up to leave.

Jumping from the bench, Mac took both her arms in his hands. "No, it's not all!" he sternly said. "We can't let it end like this. I care too much for you to see you live your life full of hate and misery."

"You care for me? Please. All you ever wanted was your damn picture. You wouldn't know how to care for anyone, Mac." Saying the name that she knew him by brought a hiccup of emotion from her. Her eyes looked down, trying to conceal the vulnerability that she felt with him.

Seeing that, Mac tenderly said, "You're wrong, Grace. I didn't plan it, didn't especially want it. But I fell in love with you—totally and completely." As he gently rubbed her arms he continued. "I've never known a woman with the generosity, the determination, the sass that you have. The first time I kissed you, I thought I'd landed in Heaven instead of Charity. You're all I could ever want." His voice was low, soft, almost like he was embarrassed to be admitting these things.

Grace's huge brown eyes were looking at him, measuring him to determine the depth of his feelings. She found herself melting in the depths of his baby blues. How did he always do that to her? Her mind was a muddled conglomeration of thoughts pulling her in different directions. "Mac," she whispered.

He pulled her into his embrace and then lowered his head to kiss her, fully, deeply, with all his heart. When Grace stiffened in his arms, he raised his head and held her away, looking at her with questioning eyes.

"Mac, I'm such a mess right now. You're really better off without me. I'm having trouble . . . I just can't seem to . . ." Grace fought against approaching tears.

"I get that Grace. But don't you see? You have the chance to fix things right now. It's time to end the hurt, the pain. Honey, Paula loves you. It's written all over her face. She's suffered long enough, don't you think?"

Grace backed away, livid. "Her name is Pauline. And I should have guessed that you wouldn't understand."

"No, no one can possibly understand the pain that you and *Pauline* have both been through. But Grace, it's not a matter of understanding anymore. It's a matter of forgiving and going on. You need to—"

"Don't say it," Grace shouted. "Don't you dare tell me what to do with my mother! Don't tell me what to do with my feelings! You think I should embrace the woman, welcome her back into my life."

"It's called being an adult," Mac said with a touch of impatience.

Enraged, Grace said, "Then I guess I'm still just a child. As a matter of fact I'm still that fifteen-year old child who misses her mother with every fiber of her being. I won't just forget the past ten years, no matter what story Pauline tells." Before the tears began to fall again in earnest, Grace began to walk away.

Mac recognized that he wasn't going to get anywhere with Grace. Disheartened, he said in a low voice, "Okay, Grace. You choose what kind of life you want to lead. I won't bother you again."

Grace stopped and looked back at Mac. Her face showed the struggle that warred in her soul. Her mouth was tight with anger and her eyes were pained with sadness. And on top of everything else, she was losing the man that she loved.

"I guess you *don't* realize the meaning of your name. What a shame." With his hands deep in his pocket, head down, he walked away.

Grace feared he walked away forever.

CHAPTER FOURTEEN

"I don't think you should be working today, honey," Ellen gently told Grace the next morning as the two women cleaned up after the breakfast rush.

Smirking, Grace said, "What else have I got to do? I'm already packed. My plane leaves day after tomorrow. There's no reason in the world that I shouldn't be here today."

Ellen noticed that no mention was made of Paula. She didn't pry. The previous evening, she had gotten Sally and Tom to take over and she had gone over to Grace's apartment. When Grace didn't open the door, Ellen used her key and walked in to find Grace curled up in a fetal position on her couch, sobbing. Undone, Ellen rushed to her and held her for hours as the girl cried more tears than any human being should ever be allowed to cry. Ellen's arms still ached. A small price to pay to comfort her niece, she thought.

"Well, you'll be here all day tomorrow. I just thought you'd like to clear up any lose ends first."

Grace's first thought was of her mother. Grace put the thought aside quickly. Nothing was going to change. She was going to New York to start a new life. One without the diner, without Charity, without Ellen, without her mother. And, sadly, one without Mac. Busying herself with organizing menus, she said, "Everything's all taken care of." Smiling slightly,

Grace looked up at her aunt. "Now you know that you don't need to babysit me tomorrow."

"Who says I'm babysitting? I'll be right here at the diner come noon for Christmas dinner with my favorite niece. You just try and stop me." Ellen said as she wiped the counter in front of Grace.

Grace knew that Ellen was putting up a brave front for her sake. She knew that Ellen hated for Grace to leave, but encouraged her to spread her wings. Precious Aunt Ellen was trying to make the best of it. Impulsively, Grace gave Ellen a one armed hug along with a peck on the cheek.

"So, after dinner here tomorrow, what are you and Howard going to do?" Grace was thankful for Howard, who she was sure would take good care of her aunt.

"We're having a quiet evening at my house. Nothing fancy." Grace smiled. "What are you smiling at?"

Having been caught, Grace quickly recovered. "I just thought it was nice that you two would have some time together, that's all."

Ellen wasn't so sure that's what the smile meant, but she wasn't going to question Grace. She was afraid that Grace's temperament was in a very delicate balance right now. In no way did she want to disturb it.

That afternoon, the bell rang over the door and in walked little Holly, her eyes sparkling with excitement. "It's Christmas Eve,

Miss Grace!" she squealed, standing by the candy counter.

Grace chuckled, walking over to her. "So it is, sweetheart. What are you doing today?"

"Well, I come by to buy my mama's Christmas present. Then I'm going to give it to her."

Conflicting emotions warred in Grace's soul. She was touched by the sweetness of the little girl's gesture, but she was also envious of her relationship with her mother. Putting a smile on her face, Grace said, "Sure, honey. What would your mama like?"

"Hmmm," Holly murmured as she looked through the candy cabinet. "I think maybe four of those chocolate malted milk balls. And one peppermint, please."

Grace smiled as she handed the sack of candy to Holly. Thinking, she said, "Holly, I've never met your mother. Has she ever been to the diner?"

"No." Holly buttoned up her coat preparing to go back outside.

"Well, why not?" Grace was very curious now. Holly was usually a very talkative child. She suddenly had become very quiet.

"She can't," Holly simply replied, not looking up at Grace.

Confused now, Grace said, "Could I meet her sometime?"

Holly looked up at Grace with shining eyes. "Oh, Miss Grace. Would you like to? Why don't you come? Right now with me."

"Go on Grace. You could use the fresh air," Ellen said wiping her hands on a towel. "Why don't you walk out with Holly? Make sure she gets home okay."

Wanting to meet Holly's mother, Grace reached for her coat. She chuckled at Holly who was jumping up and down with excitement. They walked out of the diner hand-in-hand, Ellen watching from the window.

She took a deep breath. Maybe, just maybe this was what Grace needed.

The cold wind wrapped around the pair as they walked through Charity. Grace held tight to the little girl's hand as Holly chatted away about what she and her brother were getting for Christmas. Holly led her down the road leading away from Charity. Grace thought this odd but didn't say anything. When Holly pulled her down an old dirt road off to the side, Grace stopped.

"Holly." Kneeling down to look eye-to-eye with the girl, Grace asked, "Honey are you sure that you live down this way? I don't think there are any houses down there."

"But you said you wanted to meet my mama." Holly's eyes became very sad. "Don't you still want to, Miss Grace?"

"Of course I do." She looked down the road. "Your mama is down this road?"

"Yeah. Just follow me."

Holly pulled Grace's hand and started walking down the uneven road. After about half a mile, Grace's stomach started to tighten into a big knot. There in front of her was a big gate with the words "Charity Memorial Cemetery." Grace knew the place well. It was where her father was buried. A twinge of guilt nestled into the knot in her stomach. She really should come to the gravesite sometime, maybe bring flowers.

Surprise flooded Grace's mind when Holly pulled her through the open gates of the graveyard. They walked for a while in silence, respectful of the dead. Nothing was registering in Grace's consciousness until Holly stopped in front of a modest tombstone.

And then it hit Grace.

As Holly bowed her head and took a moment to be quiet, something her father had probably taught her, Grace knelt down and read the tombstone:

Sarah Jackson
Beloved wife and mother

The date indicated that Sarah had died six months earlier, just about the time that Holly and Noel had moved to town. Grace stood up again, speechless.

After the respectable moment of silence, Holly put the small bag near the headstone. She said, "Merry Christmas, Mama." Then pointing to Grace, she said, "This is Miss Grace, the nice lady that I told you about. It's her place that I get your candy, although it won't be her place much longer. Mr. Mac bought it so I guess he'll be selling me your candy from now on."

Taking a breath, Holly looked up at Grace. The look of sorrow on Grace's face made Holly give her a little hug. "It's all right, Miss Grace. My mama wouldn't want you to be sad. She would want you to be happy."

"H-H-Holly. But your mother . . ." Grace couldn't seem to get any words out.

"I know," Holly said. "Daddy tells me she's not really there. She's in Heaven with God. But it makes me feel better to come here and talk to her. I figure because she's with God, He can make a way for her to hear me down here."

"You-you bring candy here? For her?"

"Well, of course she can't eat it. At least I don't think so. I leave it here for the animals or maybe the angels."

Grace was about undone. She didn't know what else to say; her face was contorted with a grief she rarely showed to anyone.

Holly didn't want that. "When my mama got real sick, she told me she had to go away. I cried and cried. I didn't want her to go but she dried my tears and told me that she didn't want to go away. Sometimes mamas, or daddys have to go away. Sometimes life is really hard and brings bad things. But she said that if I only thought about the bad things, I wouldn't see the good things, like candy or Christmas.

"She said that it was all right to cry when she left. I would be sad but after a while, she wanted me to look around and start noticing the good things. She wanted me to be happy because she couldn't be happy in Heaven unless I was."

Through a lump in her throat, Grace was able to smile at the wise girl and asked, "What makes you happy, Holly?"

The young girl rocked back on her heels and looked up, thinking. "Peppermints, ice cream, puppy dogs, playing with my friends, when my daddy tickles me." A bright smile came on her face. "The stars in the sky." Then looking back at her friend with barely contained excitement, Holly said, "Miss Grace, did you know that there's a Christmas star? It shines bright every year, just like it did when Jesus was born. I like to think that Mama is up there looking at the same star as I am." A thought blossoming in her mind, Holly said, "Hey, you said your daddy was one of the stars. Maybe he's next to the Christmas star. Mr. Mac told me his grandma is."

Grace thought about this as she fingered her necklace and thought about her own father looking down from heaven at her.

She felt ashamed.

Remembering Holly standing beside her, looking at her mother's grave, Grace said softly, "Holly, I'm so sorry about your mother."

"Daddy says we were really lucky to have her as long as we did."

Grace felt very ashamed.

After another few minutes of quiet, Holly said, "I've got to go home now, Miss Grace. Thanks for coming with me." Then turning to the tombstone she said, "Bye Mama. Merry Christmas. I'll see you next week."

The little girl ran off leaving a stunned Grace left alone in the cold, bitter wind.

Grace felt more alone than she had ever felt in her life. More alone than when her mother left, more alone than when her father died. Even more alone than when Mac walked away. There was a bone weary exhaustion that claimed every cell of her body. She was tired, so tired of . . . all the emotions—the hate, the frustration, the anger, the depression. She wanted so much to just live again. She wanted to be more like little Holly. She wanted to be happy.

Starting to meander through the quiet cemetery, Grace asked herself the question she had posed to Holly. What makes you happy? It was a telling thing that it took Grace a long moment before she came up with one thing. Ellen, Ellen made her happy. Accounting made her happy. A good cup of coffee in the morning, especially if it was made by Sal, made her happy. Sunrises over the lake made her happy. Fingering her star necklace, she added it to her list. All the people that came into the diner made her happy, especially the children.

Mac made her happy.

As she thought about this she wondered why she was leaving it all to go to New York City? The answer came swiftly. She was running away from memories. But wasn't that the reason she and her father had left Jacksonville? And what had happened? The memories had followed. Grace then realized that the memories would follow her anywhere. She had to deal with them here. Now.

The time to let go of the hurt had come.

But how? She thought about Holly and what she had said. Grace could hear her voice saying, "She didn't want to go away. Sometimes mamas have to go away." Isn't that what her mother had said, that she didn't have a choice but to leave?

Holly's voice kept coming back to her. "Sometimes life is really hard and brings bad things. But she said that if I only thought about the bad things, I wouldn't see the good things, like candy or Christmas."

Grace found herself walking to her father's gravesite. She needed that connection before she took the step that she knew she needed to take. As she slowly approached, a woman sat in front of the tombstone weeping. Her head was bowed, her shoulders shaking with her quiet sobs.

Her mother.

As she watched the woman, she felt another wave of shame come across her. Holly couldn't talk to a flesh and blood mother anymore. But she could. Maybe that was one of the "good things" that Holly spoke about finding.

Grace walked quietly and slowly towards her mother. She wasn't sure that she knew what to say. She fingered her necklace and stood behind the woman, waiting for inspiration.

Paula heard Grace approaching. She instinctively knew that it was her daughter. In a tear-filled voice, Paula said, "I loved him, you know."

"He loved you," Grace whispered. She walked next to Paula and sat on the cold ground leaving a few feet between them.

Sniffing into her sleeve, Paula said, "Hal was the most loveable man that I've ever known." Then with a little chuckle she added, "Even though he never remembered to put his socks in the dirty clothesbasket."

Grace looked straight ahead and said, "Yeah, I remember. He got them *to* the dirty clothesbasket, even around it. But he never could seem to get the socks in it.

"I was forever getting on to him about that." Paula looked down.

They sat quietly. Grace had no idea what to say. How strange, she thought. The woman that used to be her confidante, the woman she would run to and tell the secrets of her heart to was now a stranger. Frustration swirled through Grace along with the lingering sting of being so hurt.

Paula finally broke the silence. "Hal's Place is really nice. Did your father enjoy it?"

Did he enjoy it? Grace had to think about that. She smiled and said, "Yes, I think he did. He enjoyed all of Charity—the town, the lake, the people. Especially the people."

"That sounds just like him. He loved people, loved serving them."

More silence.

"Did Dad know about your past?" Grace asked turning to look at Paula.

Sighing, Paula said, "Yes. I told him all about it before we married. He knew that there was always a chance that the men I had been involved with would come after me." Sniffing again, she accepted a tissue that Grace handed over. "Thank you."

It was quiet again. The only sound was the wind whistling through the tall grass and the distant call of birds overhead heading south for warmer climates.

Gathering her courage, Grace said. "I think Dad would have wanted me to listen to the whole story. Why don't you start at the beginning."

Paula was so surprised; it took her a moment to gather her thoughts. Then she began telling Grace about the troubled youth she had had, how she had left Tyler, Texas as a teenager and headed to Chicago where she hooked up with a guy that she had no idea was in organized crime. By the time she understood what was going on, the man and his brother threatened her not to leave. Knowing that she couldn't live that way, she took her chances and ran south, eventually settling in Florida, where everything was wonderful for sixteen years. Until they needed her dead.

With great agony Paula told Grace how she had written the note to Hal telling him they were coming for her. She asked him to destroy the note and to love Grace for her. Both women cried.

After wandering down the coast of Florida, Paula landed in Miami, where she cleaned hotel rooms for several years until she saw Mac's ad in the paper for an assistant. Paula smiled warmly, "He took a chance on me. I'll always adore him for that." Grace thought it so like the man to help a lonely, struggling woman.

"And what about you?" Paula tentatively asked. "Tell me about Grace."

What should you tell your long-lost mother about the past ten years of your life? Grace tried to keep the pain at bay and simply state the facts. She pulled up a piece of grass and played with it as she spoke.

"Well, a year after you . . . ah, after, Dad decided that we'd move. Ellen was here in Charity and he thought it'd be perfect for us, so we came. I finished high school here." The talking was getting easier, as long as Grace didn't look into her mother's tortured eyes. "I went to the University of Florida so I could be near Dad. Got my degree in accounting, got my CPA license, and came back here to help him with Hal's Place. I figured I'd cut my teeth on keeping his books, maybe keeping the books for a few others in town, and then head up North to settle. But then Dad got sick and . . ." Her voice trailed off. Trying to speak past the big lump in her throat, Grace said, "I've been trying to sell Hal's Place ever since so I could move to New York."

"And then Mac came along," Paula added.

A flicker of tenderness shone in Grace's eyes. Then it was gone, replaced with a steady resolve. "Yes. The diner's his now so I can head to New York."

"Is that what you want?" Paula asked quietly. She had seen the love in Grace's eyes at the mention of Mac's name.

Wanting to be honest, Grace said, "I don't know any more."

Paula wanted so much to pull her daughter into her arms and hold her until the pain left, just like when she was a little girl. Her arms ached with the thought. Instead she said, "You've grown into quite a beautiful, strong woman. It's evident that everyone around here loves you very much." Then she pushed back the tears threatening to fall. "I'm very proud of you."

Something about those simple words invaded Grace's spirit. She knew that Paula was speaking her heart. Like a balm of oil poured over her head, she felt a warm sensation come over her.

But before she could embrace those warm feelings, something nagged at Grace's consciousness. "Did those men ever find you?"

Paula squeezed her eyes shut, trying not to feel the physical pain again. "Yes," she whispered. Grace waited. Paula took a deep breath. "The trial that took place ten years ago landed both of them in jail. I had hoped that meant I could go home, but my friend in Chicago told me that the contract was still out on me." Paula shivered. "I continued to hide.

"They stayed in jail for years. When they were released, they came, of all places, to Miami Beach to live." Taking a deep breath Paula continued. "One night we ran into each other. I had spent a long evening working on photographs at the studio and was heading home. The two men were coming out of a nightclub. They saw me." Paula's eyes glazed over as they looked straight ahead. "Even though it had been years, the recognition was instantaneous. They attacked me, right there, right on the street."

"No!" the sentiment was out of Grace's mouth before she even thought.

"They beat me up before the police arrived. They took off and in the process of trying to get away from the police, they crashed their car. Both of them died."

"How badly were you hurt?"

"I had a lot of bruises, a cracked rib, and a collapsed lung. I was . . . very lucky."

Grace shut her eyes as a wave of relief in her mother's safety washed over her.

"Stu, I mean Mac, came to the hospital and made sure I was given the best care available. The bruises and rib healed quickly. I still have to watch the lung."

Grace ached for the pain her mother had gone through. She didn't know what to say, how to comfort, how to make things right.

"After I knew that the two men had died, I wanted to find you and your dad. But it had been so long, I was sure that you both had gotten on with your lives. I'd just cause more problems if I showed up." Paula laughed mockingly. "What am I saying, I was just plain scared. I was a coward. I figured you were better off without me."

Grace squeezed her eyes shut hard at the pain. How could she communicate to her mother that she would never be better off without her? As the tears continued to flow, she wondered what words she could say that would bring their relationship back.

"I know it's too little too late, but Grace I am so sorry. I'm sorry for leaving. I'm sorry for not explaining it to you myself. I'm sorry for not taking you with me. I'm sorry for not trying to find you." Paula gave a humorless laugh. "I guess I'm sorry for everything about the last ten years. You deserved better and I let you down. But no matter what you may think, I do love you, Grace Anne, and I always will."

Grace couldn't speak. Her throat was so clogged with emotion she couldn't even utter a sound. She just sat there, her eyes swimming in tears, looking at her father's tombstone.

Paula interpreted Grace's silence to be unforgiveness. She held her grief inside wondering if she should just quietly leave. But no! She had to get Grace back. With the remaining strength that she possessed, she turned to face her daughter. "Those men would have found me ten years ago if I hadn't run. They would have killed you and your father," she said with a quivering voice. "If the police hadn't shown up when they did, the men would have killed me."

Grace turned to look at Paula and said softly, "I'm glad they didn't." With tears streaming down her cheeks, Grace muttered, "I've missed you, Mom."

Her eyes turning hopeful, Paula said, "I've missed you, too, baby." Then she did what she had hungered to do for the past ten years. She gathered her daughter into her arms and held her tightly. As the two women wept, Paula rocked Grace, reveling in the nearness that she thought had been lost forever. They stayed like that for a long time, neither of them noticing that night was falling and the stars were beginning to appear.

Tonight, one star was especially bright.

CHAPTER FIFTEEN

"Now, what are we going to do about Mac?" Paula said as they walked back to Charity. "Or maybe I should say, what are you going to do about Mac?" She couldn't hold back a smile.

"What do you mean?" Grace tried to ask innocently.

"Honey, I know the look in your eyes every time the man's name is mentioned. It's the same look I've always had when I think about your father." Before Grace could comment Paula continued. "I also know that you're a smart woman. You wouldn't throw away a forever kind of love."

Grace remembered a few of their conversations when she was a young adolescent. Paula liked to talk about the forever kind of love. Grace used to dream about that kind of love.

Coming back to the present, Grace said, "I don't think Mac thinks of me in those terms."

Taking Grace's arm, Paula leaned her head against her daughter's head. "Why, of course he does." Grace looked at her with a smirk. "And don't smirk at me, young lady." Grace couldn't hide a smile.

"Now you listen. I've worked with that boy for the past six years. We've worked very closely. I've seen him go out with a lot of women—some nice, some not so nice. I've seen with him with blondes, brunettes, redheads, all sizes and shapes."

"You're really not helping me feel better, here, Mom," Grace said.

"But." Paula hesitated for effect. "I've never seen him so enamored by a woman before. I've never seen him have to work so hard to get her, points to you. I've never seen him as concerned about a woman as he is about you. He bought a diner, for God sake. Who does that?"

"He just wanted to get that perfect picture."

Paula stopped and turned to look at Grace. "Honey, he already sent in the last photograph for his book. Sent it in the day before he made you the offer on the diner. He's not using the diner at all in the book."

Grace was stunned. "Then why is he buying the place?"

Paula couldn't help grinning. She'd never known two people so in love with each other and at the same time so oblivious about it. "Why don't you think about it for a minute."

"I thought it might be to get me to New York faster. That's all I ever talked about wanting and I . . ." Tears came to her eyes as she realized that Mac wanted to give her what she desired in life. At least, what he thought she desired. New York was quickly losing all appeal.

"He loves you, Grace. You must know that." Paula loved these two kids. They belonged together. She had to make sure that happened. "Why don't you tell him how you really feel about him?"

The stark reality of what had happened between them came back to Grace. "Oh, Mom. I love him, but . . . I . . . said some things. He said some things." She sighed heavily. "He'll never want me back. I've lost him."

Perfect. She's ready, Paula thought. With a smile she said, "Not if I know my partner." Then putting a finger under Grace's chin and lifting it up, she added, "And not if I know my daughter."

Determination started to come back into Grace. She loved him. She wanted him. It was time to fight for what was really important to her. Her grin matched her mother's as they started walking again.

"I think the first thing we need to do is to get his attention. Maybe we could . . . What?" Paula looked at her puzzled daughter.

Grace laughed. "You're really getting into this, aren't you?"

"You bet I am. I want grandchildren some day." Grace laughed louder. It felt so good. "Now, what do you suppose would get his attention?"

They both stopped and smiled at each other.

Mac had trouble sleeping. He tossed and turned all night. Grace would be leaving the day after Christmas. She would be on to her new life, free of the burdens of Charity.

And he was left with a diner.

How did that happen? Oh, yeah. He had wanted to help Grace, help her dreams come true. *Brilliant, Einstein. You just helped her out of your life.*

Well, that's what she chose, anyway. Although he hated that she was leaving, he hated even more that she was leaving with the same baggage that she had here. If only she would talk to Paula with an open mind. Mac worried about Paula. Her collapsed lung made it hard on her sometimes. He couldn't bear to think of the two never reconciling. Well, he'd done his best. He did everything he knew to do. Grace was so stubborn.

Grace. How was he going to go on without Grace? He had grown so accustomed to her smile in the morning, having a cup of coffee with her before the rest of Charity woke up, watching her eyes display what was going on inside of her. There was no one else like Grace.

And he was letting her go while he tried to figure out what to do with a diner. How had life become so complicated?

At about five in the morning, he gave up the pretense of sleep and crawled out of bed. After dressing, he grabbed his jacket and camera and headed outside. Maybe the cool air of the morning would revitalize him, maybe inspire him.

He walked out of the hotel's side entrance and looked at the surrounding buildings. Beautiful. It was Christmas morning. There was always something special about Christmas dawn and as he took in a big breath of the fresh morning air, he was glad he was a part of it.

Mac walked around the neighborhood closest to town, taking pictures of anything that vaguely interested him. After snapping pictures of the lit trees in the small town park, he turned to see Main Street with the lake in the background.

And he saw it.

At first he thought it was an illusion. He rubbed his eyes thinking that he definitely needed more sleep. He took a few steps closer and looked again. No, it was real! He started snapping pictures quickly, not wanting a magic moment to escape.

The sun was just peeking up behind the lake, causing an angelic glow to fall over the sleepy town. The Christmas lights on the businesses along Main Street were blazing as usual, full of holiday cheer.

And there, in the middle, in front of the lake was Hal's Place—decorated with enough lights, tinsel, garland, and ornaments to put the rest of the town to shame. There were candles in the windows. There were lights outlining the building, the doors, and the windows. Wreaths hung on every door and window. A lit nativity set was centered in the front of the building, and the bushes were filled with hundreds of colored lights. On the roof was a sleigh with eight reindeer, along with Santa and his bag of gifts— all lit up like a billboard. Across the small slope of the roof were large neon letters spelling

"Merry Christmas." It was a Christmas masterpiece.

Mac couldn't get enough of it. He kept snapping pictures. Then he noticed two lawn chairs in the road in front of the diner. Two heads could be seen above each chair, one a brunette and one a blonde. Both had a hand holding a coffee mug resting on the arm of their respective chairs. Mac's heart began to beat wildly. He got a little closer, snapping pictures as he went, and grinning a smile as bright as the rising sun.

"Well, baby, I think we did a bang-up job. What about you?" Paula asked as she rested her head against the lawn chair.

"Damn good job, Mom," Grace said taking a sip of coffee.

"Hey, watch your language. I can still wash out your mouth with soap," Paula said as she smiled at Grace.

"Sorry. Darn good job, Mom," Grace amended and she lifted her mug to Paula who tapped hers with Grace's. They both took another sip of coffee and continued to enjoy the beauty of the little diner. Both were still smiling when they heard footsteps behind them.

Mac walked up, and stopped when he was even with their lawn chairs. He just stood there looking at Hal's, his hands in his pockets, camera around his neck. He didn't say a word.

Paula and Grace looked at each other. Grace shrugged. Finally Paula said, "Well?"

"Not bad. Not bad at all," Mac said still looking at the building.

Paula knew that Grace and Mac had a lot to talk over. She stood and stretched. With a big yawn she said, "Well, I'm tuckered out. It's a good tired. I need my rest, so I think I'll just go back to the hotel and get some sleep. Thanks for the coffee, Darlin'."

"No problem. And I'll see you for dinner today?" Grace asked, standing up and taking her mother's mug.

"Absolutely. What time?"

"Twelve sharp. Right here at Hal's Place. Don't be late."

Paula chuckled. "Not a chance. Since you're doing the cooking, I'll do the cleanup. How does that sound?"

"That sounds great." Grace kissed Paula's cheek. Paula kissed her back. "Goodnight, Mom."

"Goodnight, sweetheart." Paula stroked her daughter's hair; then turned to walk away. "Goodnight, Stu. Merry Christmas."

At that moment, Grace turned to look at Mac. He was standing completely still. His eyes were bright and large, his mouth gaping at the two women. Grace couldn't help but to laugh. "Mac, what's the matter? You look a little confused."

"I think I may have stumbled upon an alternate universe. Either that or I'm dreaming."

Laughing, Grace set the coffee mugs down and walked towards him. "It's neither. It's real.

How about I pour you a cup of coffee and tell you all about it?"

Mac could hardly get his mind around what was happening. Grace, his Grace, with her sparkling brown eyes was inviting him in for coffee. After kissing her mother and telling her that she'd see her for dinner. His spirit seemed to lift as he felt for the first time that everything was really going to be all right. "I think I could use that coffee."

As they started for the diner, Grace stopped. "Oh! I almost forgot. I have one more decoration."

Mac laughed. "I don't know where you'll put anything else."

Grace reached in her back pocket and pulled out a headband. Slipping it on her head, she unfolded the top to reveal a stem coming out, holding a sprig of mistletoe. She walked close to Mac and said, "There now. The decorations are complete."

Mac's heart was bursting with happiness. He didn't know how much more he could take. With the gentleness of handling a precious gem, Mac took Grace into his arms and kissed her. Gently at first. The fire of their passion caught and soon their arms were around each other, holding and clinging to the desire of their hearts. Mac rubbed his lips over hers delighting in the cool taste and the little moans the touch incited. Grace held tight as Mac began spreading little kisses over her face, over her eyes. He moved to her neck and feasted before going back to her lips.

Between kisses, Grace whispered, "I love you, Mac. I love you so much."

"I love you too, honey," he whispered back.

"I don't want to go to New York," Grace said breathlessly. "I want to be with you. I don't care where it is, in Miami Beach, traveling around on the motorcycle. I just want you."

Mac pulled her closer and simply held her.

After a while, he said, "I think I'd just as soon settle down right here in Charity with you. Does that suit you, Grace?"

It was what Grace wanted, she realized. All the desires of her heart were coming true.

And all on Christmas Day.

EPILOGUE

ONE YEAR LATER

The town of Charity was buzzing. It was Christmas Eve and everyone was busy with preparations for the big day.

The lights of Hal's Place highlighted the Christmas decorations of the town. Amidst all the lights, wreaths, and ornaments; besides the large Santa, sleigh, and reindeer; high over the roof of the diner were three lit stars. Mac and Grace had added the star decorations in honor of Hal and Grandma McCrae and the Christmas star. It was the most popular sight in the whole town. People came from hundreds of miles to see the little diner that had captured the spirit of Christmas.

That night, the diner was extremely busy. Every seat in the house was taken and a full staff of cooks, waitresses, and busboys had been called in. Christmas music played in the background as Grace stood by the front counter which was filled with miniature Christmas villages and Christmas candy. She wore a reindeer antler headband; Mac wouldn't let her wear the mistletoe headband except alone with him in their home. She wore Christmas red and green along with large dangling Christmas ball ornament earrings. Her smile and easy laugh were as festive as the carolers that strolled the street.

Mac came in and finding his wife of ten months, planted a passionate kiss on her lips. "How's business tonight?" he asked when he came up for air.

Still a little dreamy from the kiss, she muttered, "Great. The book is selling like hotcakes."

Mac's book *Christmas in America* had been released during the Thanksgiving holidays to the delight of Mac. He hadn't been too sure that they'd get it out in time for the holidays since he had changed the cover photograph after the deadline had passed. It had all worked out and the beautiful book had smashed all selling records for its genre, topping the bestseller lists from day one.

There was a special display in Hal's Diner for the book with the cover prominently displayed. The cover photograph was of a Christmas morning in Charity. The picture showed Main Street all aglow with Hal's Diner decorated to the hilt, the sun just peeking over the lake. In the middle of the picture were two lawn chairs with two women, clicking their coffee mugs together. The picture was magic.

"Great!" Mac said as he put his arms around her waist.

"Hey, Mac. We could use some help," Noel called from the kitchen, holding a bin with dirty dishes in his arms.

"You got it." Then giving Grace a quick kiss on the cheek, Mac headed for the kitchen to start a shift as busboy.

Grace smiled at him. Imagine that—the world famous photographer Stuart McCrae bussing tables. Despite the fact that he owns the place! Grace said another prayer of thanks for her soul mate as she rang up a bill for another customer.

Paula had taken back the name of Pauline Hudson. Since her kids, Grace and Mac, now lived in Charity, she too had relocated and had taken on the job as manager of Hal's Place. Thrilled that Mac and Grace had left the name in honor of her husband, she felt like a little of him lived on in the happy diner. At the moment, she was helping out by taking orders at the counter. She had never been happier. Grace smiled widely as she watched her mother hurry around the diner.

"Hi, honey! Look's busy tonight." Ellen walked into the diner holding the hand of her handsome husband.

Howard nodded at Grace and then turned to Ellen, gently massaging the hand that he held. "I don't know if we can find a seat, sweetheart."

A contented and secretive smile forming on her lips, Ellen said, "I'll go put our order in. We can have dinner in the office." She reached up to whisper something in Howard's ear, eliciting a slight blush on his cheeks. Watching them go, Grace chuckled under her breath.

Ellen was enjoying being the wife of the mayor of Charity. She still put in time working at the diner, though not as much. Howard kept her busy as the chairperson of several service organizations, and, of course, as his wife. The mayor pampered his wife and completely adored her, which thrilled Grace. So much so, that Grace was already helping with Howard's re-election campaign.

That wasn't the only thing Grace was working on. During the year, she had taken Holly under her wing so the little girl could have a mother figure. She had also initiated monthly field trips for the Charity Elementary School to visit Hal's and began scholarship programs for high school students. Noel was already working on one.

Hal's Place was the center of the Christmas season in Charity. The diner was the hub of Christmas get-togethers, Christmas meetings, caroling, and any and every Christmas activity in Charity.

And of course, a yearly Christmas party for her beloved children was now an annual tradition with Mac playing the role of Santa Clause and then holding mistletoe over Miss Grace for a little kiss. The children loved it!

Grace smiled thinking about how much Christmas meant to her now. She looked forward to one day sharing that special feeling with her children. Looking over at the display of Mac's books, Grace grabbed one and turned to the dedication page. Her fingers lightly touched the special dedication that always brought tears to her eyes.

"To my Grace, who exemplifies all that Christmas is with her generosity, her warmth, and her love. To me and to all of us here in Charity she will forever be known as our 'Christmas Grace.'"

THE END

Play list for *Christmas Grace*

It's Beginning to Look A lot Like Christmas: by Dionne Warwick from "Miracle on 34ᵗʰ Street"

Away In A Manger: by Mannheim Steamroller from "Christmas Extraordinaire"

Frosty The Snowman: by Jimmy Durante from "A Holly Jolly Kids Christmas"

Have Yourself A Merry Little Christmas: by Kenny G from "Miracle on 34ᵗʰ Street"

The Twelve Days of Christmas: by Mitch Miller from "Holiday Sing Along with Mitch"

White Christmas: by 1,000 Strings from "1,000 Strings Play Christmas Music"

Carol of the Bells: by Return 2 Zero from "Snowfall"

Stille Nacht: by Mannheim Steamroller from "Christmas"

Christmastime is Here: by Kenny Loggins from "December"

It's the Most Wonderful Time of the Year: by Andy Williams from "The Andy Williams Christmas Album"

FORGETTING CHRISTMAS

Ali Benson didn't think she was capable of ever forgetting her favorite holiday. But when she wakes up from a car crash she discovers not only has she forgotten that it's the holiday season, but she's also forgotten the past six months of her life. Which wouldn't be so bad except for a few pertinent facts. Apparently after a whirlwind courtship, she's engaged to marry on Christmas Day!

Michael Grayson is in a hurry. He doesn't have time for the celebrations and complications of Christmas. All he wants is to marry Ali and be done with it. But in order to do that he has to keep her from remembering. Or face her rejection.

Ali and Michael deal with the season in different ways as she tries to remember and he tries to forget. But this Christmas they'll both have to confront the truth.
And hopefully find that sometimes remembering is the best part of Christmas.

Also included is the special bonus book
Sleep In Heavenly Peace Inn
Three couples at the Sleep in Heavenly Peace Inn must deal with their tumultuous relationships. With the help of three children, a man with a white beard, the inn's mysterious manager, and a reindeer, maybe they can do just that.
Available at www.amazon.com

From author Malinda Martin:

THEY BROKE UP AS KIDS. BUT MAYBE A TOY CAN BRING THEM BACK TOGETHER.

Jane Kendall has her big chance. She's been assigned to develop the marketing campaign for "CARL" the new robot computer toy that's going to take the world by storm. Everything is going great!
... until she sees the president of the toy company, which also happens to be her first love and the boy that broke her heart.

Jason Collins has worked hard for years for just this moment—the introduction of his brainchild, "CARL." The last thing he needs is the distraction of his high school sweetheart suddenly back in his life working with him. Working closely with him.

Now as the two work together for the company's promotional campaign, they discover the shocking news that the hasty wedding they had years ago after a night of drinking was never legally dissolved.   As more secrets from their past start to surface so does a burning passion that was never quite extinguished.

The Biggest Part of Me
Available now at www.amazon.com.

She'd loved him from afar and dreamed of one day meeting him. Who knew it would be in jail.

As an up and coming attorney, Julie Beaumont volunteers time as a public defender. However, she could have never guessed that one of the cases assigned to her would be defending Steven Rivers, famous singer/musician and Julie's first love. After getting him absolved of murder, she is determined to find the real murderer and clear Steven of suspicion. After all, she wants to give something back to the man that gave her years of happiness with his songs.

That's all. Nothing more. At least that's what she keeps telling herself.

Steven Rivers' life is in the gutter, and falling further until he meets a petite, brunette lawyer with fire in her eyes. Although not his normal type of woman (How come she's not falling at his feet?) Julie Beaumont intrigues him. And more. But when the actual murderer objects to Julie's investigating, he realizes that he must do more than lust after her.

It's a "whodunit" with the unlikely alliance of a forceful, conventional attorney and a celebrity singer. Together they'll find the true culprit or die trying. And in the meantime, discover feelings for each other that make the heart throb.

HEARTTHROB. Available now at www.amazon.com

Thank you so much, dear reader, for taking the time to read my story *Christmas Grace*. I'd love to hear from you! Drop me a line to say "Hi", to tell me what you thought of the story, to tell me about your favorite love stories, or all three! You can contact me at malindamartinbooks@gmail.com. Also, keep checking for upcoming books at my website www.malindamartin.com and be sure to "like" me on Facebook.

MERRY CHRISTMAS!
Malinda Martin

24912251R10133

Made in the USA
Charleston, SC
10 December 2013